Something Childish But Very Natural

KATHERINE MANSFIELD

Something Childish
But Very Natural

GREAT 🐧🐧 LOVES

To John Middleton Murry

PENGUIN BOOKS

Published by the Penguin Group
Penguin Books Ltd, 80 Strand, London WC2R 0RL, England
Penguin Group (USA) Inc., 375 Hudson Street, New York, New York 10014, USA
Penguin Group (Canada), 90 Eglinton Avenue East, Suite 700, Toronto, Ontario, Canada M4P 2Y3
(a division of Pearson Penguin Canada Inc.)
Penguin Ireland, 25 St Stephen's Green, Dublin 2, Ireland
(a division of Penguin Books Ltd)
Penguin Group (Australia), 250 Camberwell Road, Camberwell, Victoria 3124, Australia
(a division of Pearson Australia Group Pty Ltd)
Penguin Books India Pvt Ltd, 11 Community Centre, Panchsheel Park, New Delhi – 110 017, India
Penguin Group (NZ), 67 Apollo Drive, Rosedale, North Shore 0632, New Zealand
(a division of Pearson New Zealand Ltd)
Penguin Books (South Africa) (Pty) Ltd, 24 Sturdee Avenue,
Rosebank, Johannesburg 2196, South Africa

Penguin Books Ltd, Registered Offices: 80 Strand, London WC2R 0RL, England

www.penguin.com

'Feuille d'Album', 'Bliss' and 'A Dill Pickle' from *Bliss and Other Stories* first published 1920
'Mr and Mrs Dove' and 'Marriage à la Mode' from *The Garden Party and Other Stories*
first published 1923
'Honeymoon' from *The Doves' Nest and Other Stories* first published 1923
'Something Childish But Very Natural' from *Something Childish and Other Stories* first published 1924
'Widowed' from *Unfinished Stories*
This selection published in Penguin Books 2007

1

All rights reserved

Typeset by Rowland Phototypesetting Ltd, Bury St Edmunds, Suffolk
Printed in England by Clays Ltd, St Ives plc

978-0-141-03288-7

Contents

Katherine Mansfield (1888–1923) was born in Wellington, New Zealand. She came to London for the latter part of her education, and could not settle back into Wellington society; in 1908 she left for Europe again, never to return. Her first book, *In a German Pension*, was published in 1911. In 1912, she began to write for *Rhythm*, edited by John Middleton Murry, whom she eventually married. She was a conscious modernist and an experimenter in life and writing. With 'Prelude' in 1918 she established beyond doubt her distinctive voice as a writer of short fiction. By 1917 she had contracted tuberculosis, and from that time led a wandering life in search of good health. Her second book of stories, *Bliss*, was published in 1920 and her third, *The Garden Party*, appeared two years later. It was the last book to be published in her lifetime. After her death, two more collections of stories were published, as well as her *Letters*, and later, her *Journal*.

Something Childish But Very Natural

I

Whether he had forgotten what it felt like, or his head had really grown bigger since the summer before, Henry could not decide. But his straw hat hurt him: it pinched his forehead and started a dull ache in the two bones just over the temples. So he chose a corner seat in a third-class 'smoker,' took off his hat and put it in the rack with his large black cardboard portfolio and his Aunt B.'s Christmas-present gloves. The carriage smelt horribly of wet india-rubber and soot. There were ten minutes to spare before the train went, so Henry decided to go and have a look at the book-stall. Sunlight darted through the glass roof of the station in long beams of blue and gold; a little boy ran up and down carrying a tray of primroses; there was something about the people – about the women especially – something idle and yet eager. The most thrilling day of the year, the first real day of Spring had unclosed its warm delicious beauty even to London eyes. It had put a spangle in every colour and a new tone in every voice, and city folks walked as though they carried real live bodies under their clothes with real live hearts pumping the stiff blood through.

Henry was a great fellow for books. He did not read

many nor did he possess above half a dozen. He looked at all in the Charing Cross Road during lunch-time and at any odd time in London; the quantity with which he was on nodding terms was amazing. By his clean neat handling of them and by his nice choice of phrase when discussing them with one or another bookseller you would have thought that he had taken his pap with a tome propped before his nurse's bosom. But you would have been quite wrong. That was only Henry's way with everything he touched or said. That afternoon it was an anthology of English poetry, and he turned over the pages until a title struck his eye – *Something Childish But Very Natural!*

> Had I but two little wings,
> And were a little feathery bird,
> To you I'd fly, my dear,
> But thoughts like these are idle things,
> And I stay here.
>
> But in my sleep to you I fly,
> I'm always with you in my sleep,
> The world is all one's own,
> But then one wakes and where am I?
> All, all alone.
>
> Sleep stays not though a monarch bids,
> So I love to wake at break of day,
> For though my sleep be gone,
> Yet while 'tis dark one shuts one's lids,
> And so, dreams on.

He could not have done with the little poem. It was not the words so much as the whole air of it that charmed him! He might have written it lying in bed, very early in the morning, and watching the sun dance on the ceiling. 'It is *still*, like that,' thought Henry. 'I am sure he wrote it when he was half-awake some time, for it's got a smile of a dream on it.' He stared at the poem and then looked away and repeated it by heart, missed a word in the third verse and looked again and again, until he became conscious of shouting and shuffling and he looked up to see the train moving slowly.

'God's thunder!' Henry dashed forward. A man with a flag and a whistle had his hand on a door. He clutched Henry somehow . . . Henry was inside with the door slammed, in a carriage that wasn't a 'smoker,' that had not a trace of his straw hat or the black portfolio or his Aunt B.'s Christmas-present gloves. Instead, in the opposite corner, close against the wall, there sat a girl. Henry did not dare to look at her, but he felt certain she was staring at him. 'She must think I'm mad,' he thought, 'dashing into a train without even a hat, and in the evening, too.' He felt so funny. He didn't know how to sit or sprawl. He put his hands in his pockets and tried to appear quite indifferent and frown at a large photograph of Bolton Abbey. But feeling her eyes on him he gave her just the tiniest glance. Quick she looked away out of the window, and then Henry, careful of her slightest movement, went on looking. She sat pressed against the window, her cheek and shoulder half hidden by a long wave of marigold-coloured hair.

One little hand in a grey cotton glove held a leather case on her lap with the initials E. M. on it. The other hand she had slipped through the window-strap, and Henry noticed a silver bangle on the wrist with a Swiss cow-bell and a silver shoe and a fish. She wore a green coat and a hat with a wreath round it. All this Henry saw while the title of the new poem persisted in his brain – *Something Childish But Very Natural.* 'I suppose she goes to some school in London,' thought Henry. 'She might be in an office. Oh no, she is too young. Besides, she'd have her hair up if she was. It isn't even down her back.' He could not keep his eyes off that beautiful waving hair. ' "My eyes are like two drunken bees . . ." Now, I wonder if I read that or made it up?'

That moment the girl turned round and, catching his glance, she blushed. She bent her head to hide the red colour that flew in her cheeks, and Henry, terribly embarrassed, blushed too. 'I shall have to speak – have to – have to!' He started putting up his hand to raise the hat that wasn't there. He thought that funny; it gave him confidence.

'I'm – I'm most awfully sorry,' he said, smiling at the girl's hat. 'But I can't go on sitting in the same carriage with you and not explaining why I dashed in like that, without my hat even. I'm sure I gave you a fright, and just now I was staring at you – but that's only an awful fault of mine; I'm a terrible starer! If you'd like me to explain – how I got in here – not about the staring, of course,' – he gave a little laugh – 'I will.'

For a minute she said nothing, then in a low, shy voice – 'It doesn't matter.'

The train had flung behind the roofs and chimneys. They were swinging into the country, past little black woods and fading fields and pools of water shining under an apricot evening sky. Henry's heart began to thump and beat to the beat of the train. He couldn't leave it like that. She sat so quiet, hidden in her fallen hair. He felt that it was absolutely necessary that she should look up and understand him – understand him at least. He leant forward and clasped his hands round his knees.

'You see I'd just put all my things – a portfolio – into a third-class "smoker" and was having a look at the book-stall,' he explained.

As he told the story she raised her head. He saw her grey eyes under the shadow of her hat and her eyebrows like two gold feathers. Her lips were faintly parted. Almost unconsciously he seemed to absorb the fact that she was wearing a bunch of primroses and that her throat was white – the shape of her face wonderfully delicate against all that burning hair. 'How beautiful she is! How simply beautiful she is!' sang Henry's heart, and swelled with the words, bigger and bigger and trembling like a marvellous bubble – so that he was afraid to breathe for fear of breaking it.

'I hope there was nothing valuable in the portfolio,' said she, very grave.

'Oh, only some silly drawings that I was taking back from the office,' answered Henry airily. 'And – I was rather glad to lose my hat. It had been hurting me all day.'

'Yes,' she said, 'it's left a mark,' and she nearly smiled.

Why on earth should those words have made Henry feel so free suddenly and so happy and so madly excited? What was happening between them? They said nothing, but to Henry their silence was alive and warm. It covered him from his head to his feet in a trembling wave. Her marvellous words, 'It's made a mark,' had in some mysterious fashion established a bond between them. They could not be utter strangers to each other if she spoke so simply and so naturally. And now she was really smiling. The smile danced in her eyes, crept over her cheeks to her lips and stayed there. He leant back. The words flew from him – 'Isn't life wonderful!'

At that moment the train dashed into a tunnel. He heard her voice raised against the noise. She leant forward.

'I don't think so. But then I've been a fatalist for a long time now' – a pause – 'months.'

They were shattering through the dark. 'Why?' called Henry.

'Oh . . .'

Then she shrugged, and smiled and shook her head, meaning she could not speak against the noise. He nodded and leant back. They came out of the tunnel into a sprinkle of lights and houses. He waited for her to explain. But she got up and buttoned her coat and put her hands to her hat, swaying a little. 'I get out here,' she said. That seemed quite impossible to Henry.

The train slowed down and the lights outside grew brighter. She moved towards his end of the carriage.

'Look here!' he stammered. 'Shan't I see you again?' He got up too, and leant against the rack with one hand. 'I *must* see you again.' The train was stopping.

She said breathlessly, 'I come down from London every evening.'

'You – you – you do – really?' His eagerness frightened her. He was quick to curb it. Shall we or shall we not shake hands? raced through his brain. One hand was on the door-handle, the other held the little bag. The train stopped. Without another word or glance she was gone.

II

Then came Saturday – a half-day at the office – and Sunday between. By Monday evening Henry was quite exhausted. He was at the station far too early, with a pack of silly thoughts at his heels as it were driving him up and down. 'She didn't say she came by this train!' 'And supposing I go up and she cuts me.' 'There may be somebody with her.' 'Why do you suppose she's ever thought of you again?' 'What are you going to say if you do see her?' He even prayed, 'Lord, if it be Thy will, let us meet.'

But nothing helped. White smoke floated against the roof of the station – dissolved and came again in swaying wreaths. Of a sudden, as he watched it, so delicate and so silent, moving with such mysterious grace above the crowd and the scuffle, he grew calm. He felt very tired – he only wanted to sit down and shut his eyes – she was not coming – a forlorn relief breathed in the words. And then he saw her quite near to him walking towards the train with the same little leather case in her hand. Henry waited. He knew, somehow, that she had seen him, but he did not move until she came close to him and said in her low, shy voice – 'Did you get them again?'

'Oh yes, thank you, I got them again,' and with a funny half-gesture he showed her the portfolio and the gloves. They walked side by side to the train and into an empty carriage. They sat down opposite to each other, smiling timidly but not speaking, while the train moved slowly, and slowly gathered speed and smoothness. Henry spoke first.

'It's so silly,' he said, 'not knowing your name.' She put back a big piece of hair that had fallen on her shoulder, and he saw how her hand in the grey glove was shaking. Then he noticed that she was sitting very stiffly with her knees pressed together – and he was, too – both of them trying not to tremble so. She said, 'My name is Edna.'

'And mine is Henry.'

In the pause they took possession of each other's names and turned them over and put them away, a shade less frightened after that.

'I want to ask you something else now,' said Henry. He looked at Edna, his head a little on one side. 'How old are you?'

'Over sixteen,' she said, 'and you?'

'I'm nearly eighteen . . .'

'Isn't it hot?' she said suddenly, and pulled off her grey gloves and put her hands to her cheeks and kept them there. Their eyes were not frightened – they looked at each other with a sort of desperate calmness. If only their bodies would not tremble so stupidly! Still half hidden by her hair, Edna said:

'Have you ever been in love before?'

'No, never! Have you?'

'Oh, never in all my life.' She shook her head. 'I never even thought it possible.'

His next words came in a rush. 'Whatever have you been doing since last Friday evening? Whatever did you do all Saturday and all Sunday and to-day?'

But she did not answer – only shook her head and smiled and said, 'No, you tell *me*.'

'I?' cried Henry – and then he found he couldn't tell her either. He couldn't climb back to those mountains of days, and he had to shake his head too.

'But it's been agony,' he said, smiling brilliantly – 'agony.' At that she took away her hands and started laughing, and Henry joined her. They laughed until they were tired.

'It's so – so extraordinary,' she said. 'So suddenly, you know, and I feel as if I'd known you for years.'

'So do I . . .' said Henry. 'I believe it must be the Spring. I believe I've swallowed a butterfly – and it's fanning its wings just here.' He put his hand on his heart.

'And the really extraordinary thing is,' said Edna, 'that I had made up my mind that I didn't care for – men at all. I mean all the girls at College –'

'Were you at College?'

She nodded. 'A training college, learning to be a secretary.' She sounded scornful.

'I'm in an office,' said Henry. 'An architect's office – such a funny little place up one hundred and thirty stairs. We ought to be building nests instead of houses, I always think.'

'Do you like it?'

'No, of course I don't. I don't want to do anything, do you?'

'No, I hate it . . . And,' she said, 'my mother is a Hungarian – I believe that makes me hate it even more.'

That seemed to Henry quite natural. 'It would,' he said.

'Mother and I are exactly alike. I haven't a thing in common with my father; he's just . . . a little man in the City – but mother has got wild blood in her and she's given it to me. She hates our life just as much as I do.' She paused and frowned. 'All the same, we don't get on a bit together – that's funny – isn't it? But I'm absolutely alone at home.'

Henry was listening – in a way he was listening, but there was something else he wanted to ask her. He said, very shyly, 'Would you – would you take off your hat?'

She looked startled. 'Take off my hat?'

'Yes – it's your hair. I'd give anything to see your hair properly.'

She protested. 'It isn't really . . .'

'Oh, it *is*,' cried Henry, and then, as she took off the hat and gave her head a little toss, 'Oh, Edna! it's the loveliest thing in the world.'

'Do you like it?' she said, smiling and very pleased. She pulled it round her shoulders like a cape of gold.

'People generally laugh at it. It's such an absurd colour.' But Henry would not believe that. She leaned her elbows on her knees and cupped her chin in her hands. 'That's how I often sit when I'm angry and then I feel it burning me up . . . Silly?'

'No, no, not a bit,' said Henry. 'I knew you did. It's your sort of weapon against all the dull horrid things.'

'However did you know that? Yes, that's just it. But however did you know?'

'Just knew,' smiled Henry. 'My God!' he cried, 'what fools people are! All the little pollies that you know and that I know. Just look at you and me. Here we are – that's all there is to be said. I know about you and you know about me – we've just found each other – quite simply – just by being natural. That's all life is – something childish and very natural. Isn't it?'

'Yes – yes,' she said eagerly. 'That's what I've always thought.'

'It's people that make things so – silly. As long as you can keep away from them you're safe and you're happy.'

'Oh, I've thought that for a long time.'

'Then you're just like me,' said Henry. The wonder of that was so great that he almost wanted to cry. Instead he said very solemnly: 'I believe we're the only two people alive who think as we do. In fact, I'm sure of it. Nobody understands me. I feel as though I were living in a world of strange beings – do you?'

'Always.'

'We'll be in that loathsome tunnel again in a minute,' said Henry. 'Edna! can I – just touch your hair?'

She drew back quickly. 'Oh no, please don't,' and as they were going into the dark she moved a little away from him.

III

'Edna! I've bought the tickets. The man at the concert hall didn't seem at all surprised that I had the money. Meet me outside the gallery doors at three, and wear that cream blouse and the corals – will you? I love you. I don't like sending these letters to the shop. I always feel those people with "Letters received" in their window keep a kettle in their back parlour that would steam open an elephant's ear of an envelope. But it really doesn't matter, does it, darling? Can you get away on Sunday? Pretend you are going to spend the day with one of the girls from the office, and let's meet at some little place and walk or find a field where we can watch the daisies uncurling. I do love you, Edna. But Sundays without you are simply impossible. Don't get run over before Saturday, and don't eat anything out of a tin or drink anything from a public fountain. That's all, darling.'

'My dearest, yes, I'll be there on Saturday – and I've arranged about Sunday too. That is one great blessing. I'm quite free at home. I have just come in from the garden. It's such a lovely evening. Oh, Henry, I could sit and cry, I love you so to-night. Silly – isn't it? I either

*feel so happy I can hardly stop laughing or else so sad I
can hardly stop crying, and both for the same reason. But
we are so young to have found each other, aren't we? I
am sending you a violet. It is quite warm. I wish you
were here now, just for a minute even. Good-night,
darling. – I am, Edna.'*

IV

'Safe,' said Edna, 'safe! And excellent places, aren't
they, Henry?'

She stood up to take off her coat and Henry made a
movement to help her. 'No – no – it's off.' She tucked
it under the seat. She sat down beside him. 'Oh, Henry,
what have you got there? Flowers?'

'Only two tiny little roses.' He laid them in her lap.

'Did you get my letter all right?' asked Edna,
unpinning the paper.

'Yes,' he said, 'and the violet is growing beautifully.
You should see my room. I planted a little piece of it
in every corner and one on my pillow and one in the
pocket of my pyjama jacket.'

She shook her hair at him. 'Henry, give me the
programme.'

'Here it is – you can read it with me. I'll hold it for
you.'

'No, let me have it.'

'Well, then, I'll read it for you.'

'No, you can have it after.'

'Edna,' he whispered.

'Oh, please don't,' she pleaded. 'Not here – the people.'

Why did he want to touch her so much and why did she mind? Whenever he was with her he wanted to hold her hand or take her arm when they walked together, or lean against her – not hard – just lean lightly so that his shoulder should touch her shoulder – and she wouldn't even have that. All the time that he was away from her he was hungry, he craved the nearness of her. There seemed to be comfort and warmth breathing from Edna that he needed to keep him calm. Yes, that was it. He couldn't get calm with her because she wouldn't let him touch her. But she loved him. He knew that. Why did she feel so curiously about it? Every time he tried to or even asked for her hand she shrank back and looked at him with pleading, frightened eyes as though he wanted to hurt her. They could say anything to each other. And there wasn't any question of their belonging to each other. And yet he couldn't touch her. Why, he couldn't even help her off with her coat. Her voice dropped into his thoughts.

'Henry!' He leaned to listen, setting his lips. 'I want to explain something to you. I will – I will – I promise – after the concert.'

'All right.' He was still hurt.

'You're not sad, are you?' she said.

He shook his head.

'Yes, you are, Henry.'

'No, really not.' He looked at the roses lying in her hands.

'Well, are you happy?'

'Yes. Here comes the orchestra.'

It was twilight when they came out of the hall. A blue net of light hung over the streets and houses, and pink clouds floated in a pale sky. As they walked away from the hall Henry felt they were very little and alone. For the first time since he had known Edna his heart was heavy.

'Henry!' She stopped suddenly and stared at him. 'Henry, I'm not coming to the station with you. Don't – don't wait for me. Please, please leave me.'

'My God!' cried Henry, and started, 'what's the matter – Edna – darling – Edna, what have I done?'

'Oh, nothing – go away,' and she turned and ran across the street into a square and leaned up against the square railings – and hid her face in her hands.

'Edna – Edna – my little love – you're crying. Edna, my baby girl!'

She leaned her arms along the railings and sobbed distractedly.

'Edna – stop – it's all my fault. I'm a fool – I'm a thundering idiot. I've spoiled your afternoon. I've tortured you with my idiotic mad bloody clumsiness. That's it. Isn't it, Edna? For God's sake.'

'Oh,' she sobbed, 'I do hate hurting you so. Every time you ask me to let – let you hold my hand or – or kiss me I could kill myself for not doing it – for not letting you. I don't know why I don't even.' She said wildly, 'It's not that I'm frightened of you – it's not that – it's only a feeling, Henry, that I can't understand myself even. Give me your handkerchief, darling.' He pulled it from his pocket. 'All through the concert I've been haunted by this, and every time we meet I know it's bound to come up. Somehow I feel if once we did that – you know – held each other's hands and kissed, it would be all changed – and I feel we wouldn't be free like we are – we'd be doing something secret. We wouldn't be children any more . . . silly, isn't it? I'd feel awkward with you, Henry, and I'd feel shy, and I do so feel that just because you and I are you and I, we don't need that sort of thing.' She turned and looked at him, pressing her hands to her cheeks in the way he knew so well, and behind her as in a dream he saw the sky and half a white moon and the trees of the square with their unbroken buds. He kept twisting, twisting up in his hands the concert programme. 'Henry! You do understand me – don't you?'

'Yes, I think I do. But you're not going to be frightened any more, are you?' He tried to smile. 'We'll forget, Edna. I'll never mention it again. We'll bury the bogy in this square – now – you and I – won't we?'

'But,' she said, searching his face – 'will it make you love me less?'

'Oh no,' he said. 'Nothing could – nothing on earth could do that.'

V

London became their playground. On Saturday afternoons they explored. They found their own shops where they bought cigarettes and sweets for Edna –

and their own tea-shop with their own table – their own streets – and one night when Edna was supposed to be at a lecture at the Polytechnic they found their own village. It was the name that made them go there. 'There's white geese in that name,' said Henry, telling it to Edna. 'And a river and little low houses with old men sitting outside them – old sea captains with wooden legs winding up their watches, and there are little shops with lamps in the windows.'

It was too late for them to see the geese or the old men, but the river was there and the houses and even the shops with lamps. In one a woman sat working a sewing-machine on the counter. They heard the whirring hum and they saw her big shadow filling the shop. 'Too full for a single customer,' said Henry. 'It is a perfect place.'

The houses were small and covered with creepers and ivy. Some of them had worn wooden steps leading up to the doors. You had to go down a little flight of steps to enter some of the others; and just across the road – to be seen from every window – was the river, with a walk beside it and some high poplar trees.

'This is the place for us to live in,' said Henry. 'There's a house to let, too. I wonder if it would wait if we asked it. I'm sure it would.'

'Yes, I would like to live there,' said Edna. They crossed the road and she leaned against the trunk of a tree and looked up at the empty house with a dreamy smile.

'There is a little garden at the back, dear,' said Henry, 'a lawn with one tree on it and some daisy bushes round the wall. At night the stars shine in the tree like tiny candles. And inside there are two rooms downstairs and a big room with folding doors upstairs and above that an attic. And there are eight stairs to the kitchen – very dark, Edna. You are rather frightened of them, you know. "Henry, dear, would you mind bringing the lamp? I just want to make sure that Euphemia has raked out the fire before we go to bed."'

'Yes,' said Edna. 'Our bedroom is at the very top – that room with the two square windows. When it is quiet we can hear the river flowing and the sound of the poplar trees far, far away, rustling and flowing in our dreams, darling.'

'You're not cold – are you?' he said suddenly.

'No – no, only happy.'

'The room with the folding doors is yours.' Henry laughed. 'It's a mixture – it isn't a room at all. It's full of your toys and there's a big blue chair in it where you sit curled up in front of the fire with the flames in your curls – because though we're married you refuse to put your hair up and only tuck it inside your coat for the church service. And there's a rug on the floor for me to lie on, because I'm so lazy. Euphemia – that's our servant – only comes in the day. After she's gone we go down to the kitchen and sit on the table and eat an apple, or perhaps we make some tea, just for the sake of hearing the kettle sing. That's not joking. If you listen to a kettle right through it's like an early morning in Spring.'

'Yes, I know,' she said. 'All the different kinds of birds.'

A little cat came through the railings of the empty house and into the road. Edna called it and bent down and held out her hands – 'Kitty! Kitty!' The little cat ran to her and rubbed against her knees.

'If we're going for a walk just take the cat and put it inside the front door,' said Henry, still pretending. 'I've got the key.'

They walked across the road and Edna stood stroking the cat in her arms while Henry went up the steps and pretended to open the door.

He came down again quickly. 'Let's go away at once. It's going to turn into a dream.'

The night was dark and warm. They did not want to go home. 'What I feel so certain of is,' said Henry, 'that we ought to be living there now. We oughtn't to wait for things. What's age? You're as old as you'll ever be and so am I. You know,' he said, 'I have a feeling often and often that it's dangerous to wait for things – that if you wait for things they only go further and further away.'

'But, Henry, – money! You see we haven't any money.'

'Oh, well, – perhaps if I disguised myself as an old man we could get a job as caretakers in some large house – that would be rather fun. I'd make up a terrific history of the house if anyone came to look over it, and you could dress up and be the ghost moaning and wringing your hands in the deserted picture gallery, to frighten them off. Don't you ever feel that money is more or less accidental – that if one really wants things it's either there or it doesn't matter?'

She did not answer that – she looked up at the sky and said, 'Oh dear, I don't want to go home.'

'Exactly – that's the whole trouble – and we oughtn't to go home. We ought to be going back to the house and find an odd saucer to give the cat the dregs of the milk-jug in. I'm not really laughing – I'm not even happy. I'm lonely for you, Edna – I would give anything to lie down and cry' . . . and he added limply, 'with my head in your lap and your darling cheek in my hair.'

'But, Henry,' she said, coming closer, 'you have faith, haven't you? I mean you are absolutely certain that we shall have a house like that and everything we want – aren't you?'

'Not enough – that's not enough. I want to be sitting on those very stairs and taking off these very boots this very minute. Don't you? Is faith enough for you?'

'If only we weren't so young . . .' she said miserably. 'And yet,' she sighed, 'I'm sure I don't feel very young – I feel twenty at least.'

VI

Henry lay on his back in the little wood. When he moved the dead leaves rustled beneath him, and above his head the new leaves quivered like fountains of green water steeped in sunlight. Somewhere out of sight Edna was gathering primroses. He had been so full of dreams that morning that he could not keep pace with her delight in the flowers. 'Yes, love, you go and come back for me. I'm too lazy.' She had thrown off her hat and knelt down beside him, and by and by her voice and her footsteps had grown fainter. Now the wood was silent except for the leaves, but he knew that she was not far away and he moved so that the tips of his fingers touched her pink jacket. Ever since waking he had felt so strangely that he was not really awake at all, but just dreaming. The time before Edna was a dream, and now he and she were dreaming together and somewhere in some dark place another dream waited for him. 'No, that can't be true because I can't ever imagine the world without us. I feel that we two together mean something that's got to be there just as naturally as trees or birds or clouds.' He tried to remember what it had felt like without Edna, but he could not get back to those days. They were hidden by her; Edna with the marigold hair and strange, dreamy smile filled him up to the brim. He breathed her; he ate and drank her. He walked about with a shining ring of Edna keeping the world away or touching whatever it lighted on with its own beauty. 'Long after you have stopped laughing,' he told her, 'I can hear your laugh running up and down my veins – and yet – are we a dream?' And suddenly he saw himself and Edna as two very small children walking through the streets, looking through windows, buying things and playing with them, talking to each other, smiling – he saw even their gestures and the way they stood, so often, quite still, face to face – and then he rolled over and pressed his face in the leaves – faint with longing. He wanted to kiss Edna, and to put his arms round her and press her to him and feel her cheek hot against his kiss, and kiss her until he'd no breath left and so stifle the dream.

'No, I can't go on being hungry like this,' said Henry, and jumped up and began to run in the direction she had gone. She had wandered a long way. Down in a green hollow he saw her kneeling, and when she saw him she waved and said – 'Oh, Henry – such beauties! I've never seen such beauties. Come and look.' By the time he had reached her he would have cut off his hand rather than spoil her happiness. How strange Edna was that day! All the time she talked to Henry her eyes laughed; they were sweet and mocking. Two little spots of colour like strawberries glowed on her cheeks and 'I wish I could feel tired,' she kept saying. 'I want to walk over the whole world until I die. Henry – come along. Walk faster – Henry! If I start flying suddenly, you'll promise to catch hold of my feet, won't you? Otherwise I'll never come down.' And 'Oh,' she cried, 'I am so happy. I'm so frightfully happy!' They came to a weird place, covered with heather. It was early afternoon and the sun streamed down upon the purple.

'Let's rest here a little,' said Edna, and she waded into the heather and lay down. 'Oh, Henry, it's so lovely. I can't see anything except the little bells and the sky.'

Henry knelt down by her and took some primroses out of her basket and made a long chain to go round her throat. 'I could almost fall asleep,' said Edna. She crept over to his knees and lay hidden in her hair just beside him. 'It's like being under the sea, isn't it, dearest, so sweet and so still?'

'Yes,' said Henry, in a strange, husky voice. 'Now I'll make you one of violets.' But Edna sat up. 'Let's go in,' she said.

They came back to the road and walked a long way. Edna said, 'No, I couldn't walk over the world – I'm tired now.' She trailed on the grass edge of the road. 'You and I are tired, Henry! How much further is it?'

'I don't know – not very far,' said Henry, peering into the distance. Then they walked in silence.

'Oh,' she said at last, 'it really is too far, Henry, I'm tired and I'm hungry. Carry my silly basket of primroses.' He took them without looking at her.

At last they came to a village and a cottage with a notice 'Teas Provided.'

'This is the place,' said Henry. 'I've often been here. You sit on the little bench and I'll go and order the tea.' She sat down on the bench, in the pretty garden all white and yellow with spring flowers. A woman came to the door and leaned against it watching them eat. Henry was very nice to her, but Edna did not say a word. 'You haven't been here for a long spell,' said the woman.

'No – the garden's looking wonderful.'

'Fair,' said she. 'Is the young lady your sister?' Henry nodded Yes, and took some jam.

'There's a likeness,' said the woman. She came down into the garden and picked a head of white jonquils and handed it to Edna. 'I suppose you don't happen to know anyone who wants a cottage,' said she. 'My sister's taken ill and she left me hers. I want to let it.'

'For a long time?' asked Henry politely.

'Oh,' said the woman vaguely, 'that depends.'

Said Henry, 'Well – I might know of somebody – could we go and look at it?'

'Yes, it's just a step down the road, the little one with the apple trees in front – I'll fetch you the key.'

While she was away Henry turned to Edna and said, 'Will you come?' She nodded.

They walked down the road and in through the gate and up the grassy path between the pink and white trees. It was a tiny place – two rooms downstairs and two rooms upstairs. Edna leaned out of the top window, and Henry stood at the doorway. 'Do you like it?' he asked.

'Yes,' she called, and then made a place for him at the window. 'Come and look. It's so sweet.'

He came and leant out of the window. Below them were the apple trees tossing in a faint wind that blew a long piece of Edna's hair across his eyes. They did not move. It was evening – the pale green sky was sprinkled with stars. 'Look!' she said – 'stars, Henry.'

'There will be a moon in two T's,' said Henry.

She did not seem to move and yet she was leaning against Henry's shoulder; he put his arm round her – 'Are all those trees down there – apple?' she asked in a shaky voice.

'No, darling,' said Henry. 'Some of them are full of angels and some of them are full of sugar almonds – but evening light is awfully deceptive.' She sighed. 'Henry – we mustn't stay here any longer.'

He let her go and she stood up in the dusky room and touched her hair. 'What has been the matter with you all day?' she said – and then did not wait for an answer but ran to him and put her arms round his neck, and pressed his head into the hollow of her shoulder. 'Oh,' she breathed, 'I do love you. Hold me, Henry.' He put his arms round her, and she leaned against him and looked into his eyes. 'Hasn't it been terrible, all to-day?' said Edna. 'I knew what was the matter and I've tried every way I could to tell you that I wanted you to kiss me – that I'd quite got over the feeling.'

'You're perfect, perfect, perfect,' said Henry.

VII

'The thing is,' said Henry, 'how am I going to wait until evening?' He took his watch out of his pocket, went into the cottage and popped it into a china jar on the mantelpiece. He'd looked at it seven times in one hour, and now he couldn't remember what time it was. Well, he'd look once again. Half-past four. Her train arrived at seven. He'd have to start for the station at half-past six. Two hours more to wait. He went through the cottage again – downstairs and upstairs. 'It looks lovely,' he said. He went into the garden and picked a round bunch of white pinks and put them in a vase on the little table by Edna's bed. 'I don't believe this,' thought Henry. 'I don't believe this for a minute. It's too much. She'll be here in two hours and we'll walk home, and then I'll take that white jug off the kitchen table and go across to Mrs Biddie's and get the milk, and then come back, and when I come back she'll have lighted the lamp in the kitchen and I'll look through the window and see her moving about in the pool of lamplight. And then we shall have supper, and after supper (Bags I washing up!) I shall put some wood on the fire and we'll sit on the hearth-rug and watch it burning. There won't be a sound except the wood and perhaps the wind will creep round the house once . . . And then we shall light our candles and she will go up first with her shadow on the wall beside her, and she will call out, Good-night, Henry – and I shall answer – Goodnight, Edna. And then I shall dash upstairs and jump into bed and watch the tiny bar of light from her room brush my door, and the moment it disappears will shut my eyes and sleep until morning. Then we'll have all to-morrow and to-morrow and to-morrow night. Is she thinking all this, too? Edna, come quickly!

> Had I but two little wings,
> And were a little feathery bird,
> To you I'd fly, my dear –

'No, no, dearest . . . Because the waiting is a sort of Heaven, too, darling. If you can understand that. Did you ever know a cottage could stand on tiptoe. This one is doing it now.'

He was downstairs and sat on the doorstep with his hands clasped round his knees. That night when they found the village – and Edna said, 'Haven't you faith, Henry?' 'I hadn't then. Now I have,' he said, 'I feel just like God.'

He leaned his head against the lintel. He could hardly keep his eyes open, not that he was sleepy, but . . . for some reason . . . and a long time passed.

Henry thought he saw a big white moth flying down the road. It perched on the gate. No, it wasn't a moth. It was a little girl in a pinafore. What a nice little girl, and he smiled in his sleep, and she smiled, too, and turned in her toes as she walked. 'But she can't be living here,' thought Henry. 'Because this is ours. Here she comes.'

When she was quite close to him she took her hand from under her pinafore and gave him a telegram and smiled and went away. There's a funny present! thought Henry, staring at it. 'Perhaps it's only a make-believe one, and it's got one of those snakes inside it that fly up at you.' He laughed gently in the dream and opened it very carefully. 'It's just a folded paper.' He took it out and spread it open.

The garden became full of shadows – they spun a web of darkness over the cottage and the trees and Henry and the telegram. But Henry did not move.

Feuille d'Album

He really was an impossible person. Too shy altogether. With absolutely nothing to say for himself. And such a weight. Once he was in your studio he never knew when to go, but would sit on and on until you nearly screamed, and burned to throw something enormous after him when he did finally blush his way out – something like the tortoise stove. The strange thing was that at first sight he looked most interesting. Everybody agreed about that. You would drift into the café one evening and there you would see, sitting in a corner, with a glass of coffee in front of him, a thin, dark boy, wearing a blue jersey with a little grey flannel jacket buttoned over it. And somehow that blue jersey and the grey jacket with the sleeves that were too short gave him the air of a boy that has made up his mind to run away to sea. Who has run away, in fact, and will get up in a moment and sling a knotted handkerchief containing his nightshirt and his mother's picture on the end of a stick, and walk out into the night and be drowned . . . Stumble over the wharf edge on his way to the ship, even . . . He had black close-cropped hair, grey eyes with long lashes, white cheeks and a mouth pouting as though he were determined not to cry . . . How could one resist him? Oh, one's heart was wrung at sight. And, as if that were not enough, there was his trick of blushing . . . Whenever the waiter came near him he turned crimson – he might have been just out of prison and the waiter in the know . . .

'Who is he, my dear? Do you know?'

'Yes. His name is Ian French. Painter. Awfully clever, they say. Someone started by giving him a mother's tender care. She asked him how often he heard from home, whether he had enough blankets on his bed, how much milk he drank a day. But when she went round to his studio to give an eye to his socks, she rang and rang, and though she could have sworn she heard someone breathing inside, the door was not answered . . . Hopeless!'

Someone else decided that he ought to fall in love. She summoned him to her side, called him 'boy,' leaned over him so that he might smell the enchanting perfume of her hair, took his arm, told him how marvellous life could be if one only had the courage, and went round to his studio one evening and rang and rang . . . Hopeless.

'What the poor boy really wants is thoroughly rousing,' said a third. So off they went to cafés and cabarets, little dances, places where you drank something that tasted like tinned apricot juice, but cost twenty-seven shillings a bottle and was called champagne, other places, too thrilling for words, where you sat in the most awful gloom, and where someone had always been shot the night before. But he did not turn a hair. Only once he got very drunk, but instead of blossoming forth, there he sat, stony, with two spots of red on his cheeks, like, my dear, yes, the dead image of that

rag-time thing they were playing, like a 'Broken Doll.'
But when she took him back to his studio he had quite
recovered, and said 'good night' to her in the street
below, as though they had walked home from church
together . . . Hopeless.

After heaven knows how many more attempts – for
the spirit of kindness dies very hard in women – they
gave him up. Of course, they were still perfectly charming, and asked him to their shows, and spoke to him
in the café, but that was all. When one is an artist one
has no time simply for people who won't respond.
Has one?

'And besides I really think there must be something
rather fishy somewhere . . . don't you? It can't all be as
innocent as it looks! Why come to Paris if you want to
be a daisy in the field? No, I'm not suspicious. But –'

He lived at the top of a tall mournful building overlooking the river. One of those buildings that look so
romantic on rainy nights and moonlight nights, when
the shutters are shut, and the heavy door, and the
sign advertising 'a little apartment to let immediately'
gleams forlorn beyond words. One of those buildings
that smell so unromantic all the year round, and where
the concierge lives in a glass cage on the ground floor,
wrapped up in a filthy shawl, stirring something in a
saucepan and ladling out tit-bits to the swollen old dog
lolling on a bead cushion . . . Perched up in the air the
studio had a wonderful view. The two big windows
faced the water; he could see the boats and the barges
swinging up and down, and the fringe of an island
planted with trees, like a round bouquet. The side

window looked across to another house, shabbier still
and smaller, and down below there was a flower market.
You could see the tops of huge umbrellas, with frills of
bright flowers escaping from them, booths covered
with striped awning where they sold plants in boxes
and clumps of wet gleaming palms in terracotta jars.
Among the flowers the old women scuttled from side
to side, like crabs. Really there was no need for him to
go out. If he sat at the window until his white beard
fell over the sill he still would have found something
to draw . . .

How surprised those tender women would have been
if they had managed to force the door. For he kept his
studio as neat as a pin. Everything was arranged to
form a pattern, a little 'still life' as it were – the sauce-
pans with their lids on the wall behind the gas stove,
the bowl of eggs, milk-jug and teapot on the shelf, the
books and the lamp with the crinkly paper shade on
the table. An Indian curtain that had a fringe of red
leopards marching round it covered his bed by day, and
on the wall beside the bed on a level with your eyes
when you were lying down there was a small neatly
printed notice: GET UP AT ONCE.

Every day was much the same. While the light was
good he slaved at his painting, then cooked his meals
and tidied up the place. And in the evenings he went
off to the café, or sat at home reading or making out
the most complicated list of expenses headed: 'What I
ought to be able to do it on,' and ending with a sworn
statement . . . 'I swear not to exceed this amount for
next month. Signed, Ian French.'

Nothing very fishy about this; but those far-seeing women were quite right. It wasn't all.

One evening he was sitting at the side window eating some prunes and throwing the stones on to the tops of the huge umbrellas in the deserted flower market. It had been raining – the first real spring rain of the year had fallen – a bright spangle hung on everything, and the air smelled of buds and moist earth. Many voices sounding languid and content rang out in the dusky air, and the people who had come to close their windows and fasten the shutters leaned out instead. Down below in the market the trees were peppered with new green. What kind of trees were they? he wondered. And now came the lamplighter. He stared at the house across the way, the small, shabby house, and suddenly, as if in answer to his gaze, two wings of windows opened and a girl came out on to the tiny balcony carrying a pot of daffodils. She was a strangely thin girl in a dark pinafore, with a pink handkerchief tied over her hair. Her sleeves were rolled up almost to her shoulders and her slender arms shone against the dark stuff.

'Yes, it is quite warm enough. It will do them good,' she said, putting down the pot and turning to someone in the room inside. As she turned she put her hands up to the handkerchief and tucked away some wisps of hair. She looked down at the deserted market and up at the sky, but where he sat there might have been a hollow in the air. She simply did not see the house opposite. And then she disappeared.

His heart fell out of the side window of his studio,

and down to the balcony of the house opposite – buried itself in the pot of daffodils under the half-opened buds and spears of green ... That room with the balcony was the sitting-room, and the one next door to it was the kitchen. He heard the clatter of the dishes as she washed up after supper, and then she came to the window, knocked a little mop against the ledge, and hung it on a nail to dry. She never sang or unbraided her hair, or held out her arms to the moon as young girls are supposed to do. And she always wore the same dark pinafore and the pink handkerchief over her hair ... Whom did she live with? Nobody else came to those two windows, and yet she was always talking to someone in the room. Her mother, he decided, was an invalid. They took in sewing. The father was dead ... He had been a journalist – very pale, with long moustaches, and a piece of black hair falling over his forehead.

By working all day they just made enough money to live on, but they never went out and they had no friends. Now when he sat down at his table he had to make an entirely new set of sworn statements ... Not to go to the side window before a certain hour: signed, Ian French. Not to think about her until he had put away his painting things for the day: signed, Ian French.

It was quite simple. She was the only person he really wanted to know, because she was, he decided, the only other person alive who was just his age. He couldn't stand giggling girls, and he had no use for grown-up women ... She was his age, she was – well, just like him. He sat in his dusky studio, tired, with one arm hanging over the back of his chair, staring in at her window and seeing himself in there with her. She had a violent temper; they quarrelled terribly at times, he and she. She had a way of stamping her foot and twisting her hands in her pinafore . . . furious. And she very rarely laughed. Only when she told him about an absurd little kitten she once had who used to roar and pretend to be a lion when it was given meat to eat. Things like that made her laugh . . . But as a rule they sat together very quietly; he, just as he was sitting now, and she with her hands folded in her lap and her feet tucked under, talking in low tones, or silent and tired after the day's work. Of course, she never asked him about his pictures, and of course he made the most wonderful drawings of her which she hated, because he made her so thin and so dark . . . But how could he get to know her? This might go on for years . . .

Then he discovered that once a week, in the evenings, she went out shopping. On two successive Thursdays she came to the window wearing an old-fashioned cape over the pinafore, and carrying a basket. From where he sat he could not see the door of her house, but on the next Thursday evening at the same time he snatched up his cap and ran down the stairs. There was a lovely pink light over everything. He saw it glowing in the river, and the people walking towards him had pink faces and pink hands.

He leaned against the side of his house waiting for her and he had no idea of what he was going to do or say. 'Here she comes,' said a voice in his head. She walked very quickly, with small, light steps; with one hand she carried the basket, with the other she kept the cape together ... What could he do? He could only follow ... First she went into the grocer's and spent a long time in there, and then she went into the butcher's where she had to wait her turn. Then she was an age at the draper's matching something, and then she went to the fruit shop and bought a lemon. As he watched her he knew more surely than ever he must get to know her, now. Her composure, her seriousness and her loneliness, the very way she walked as though she was eager to be done with this world of grown-ups, all was so natural to him and so inevitable.

'Yes, she is always like that,' he thought proudly. 'We have nothing to do with these people.'

But now she was on her way home and he was as far off as ever ... She suddenly turned into the dairy and he saw her through the window buying an egg. She picked it out of the basket with such care – a brown one, a beautifully shaped one, the one he would have chosen. And when she came out of the dairy he went in after her. In a moment he was out again, and following her past his house across the flower market, dodging among the huge umbrellas and treading on the fallen flowers and the round marks where the pots had stood ... Through her door he crept, and up the stairs after, taking care to tread in time with her so that she should not notice. Finally, she stopped on the landing, and took the key out of her purse. As she put it into the door he ran up and faced her.

Blushing more crimson than ever, but looking at

her severely, he said, almost angrily: 'Excuse me, Mademoiselle, you dropped this.'

And he handed her an egg.

Mr and Mrs Dove

Of course he knew – no man better – that he hadn't a ghost of a chance, he hadn't an earthly. The very idea of such a thing was preposterous. So preposterous that he'd perfectly understand it if her father – well, whatever her father chose to do he'd perfectly understand. In fact, nothing short of desperation, nothing short of the fact that this was positively his last day in England for God knows how long, would have screwed him up to it. And even now . . . He chose a tie out of the chest of drawers, a blue and cream check tie, and sat on the side of his bed. Supposing she replied, 'What impertinence!' would he be surprised? Not in the least, he decided, turning up his soft collar and turning it down over the tie. He expected her to say something like that. He didn't see, if he looked at the affair dead soberly, what else she could say.

Here he was! And nervously he tied a bow in front of the mirror, jammed his hair down with both hands, pulled out the flaps of his jacket pockets. Making between £500 and £600 a year on a fruit farm in – of all places – Rhodesia. No capital. Not a penny coming to him. No chance of his income increasing for at least four years. As for looks and all that sort of thing, he was completely out of the running. He couldn't even boast of top-hole health, for the East Africa business had knocked him out so thoroughly that he'd had to take six months' leave. He was still fearfully pale – worse even than usual this afternoon, he thought, bending forward and peering into the mirror. Good heavens! What had happened? His hair looked almost bright green. Dash it all, he hadn't green hair, at all events. That was a bit too steep. And then the green light trembled in the glass; it was the shadow from the tree outside. Reggie turned away, took out his cigarette-case, but remembering how the mater hated him to smoke in his bedroom, put it back again and drifted over to the chest of drawers. No, he was dashed if he could think of one blessed thing in his favour, while she . . . Ah! . . . He stopped dead, folded his arms, and leaned hard against the chest of drawers.

And in spite of her position, her father's wealth, the fact that she was an only child and far and away the most popular girl in the neighbourhood; in spite of her beauty and her cleverness – cleverness! – it was a great deal more than that – there was really nothing she couldn't do; he fully believed, had it been necessary, she would have been a genius at anything – in spite of the fact that her parents adored her, and she them, and they'd as soon let her go all that way as . . . In spite of every single thing you could think of, so terrific was his love that he couldn't help hoping. Well, was it hope? Or was this queer, timid longing to have the chance of looking after her, of making it his job to see that she had everything she wanted, and that nothing came near her that wasn't perfect – just love? How he loved her! He squeezed hard against the chest of drawers and murmured to it, 'I love her, I love her!' And just for the moment he was with her on the way to Umtali. It was night. She sat in a corner asleep. Her soft chin was tucked into her soft collar, her gold-brown lashes lay on her cheeks. He doted on her delicate little nose, her perfect lips, her ear like a baby's and the gold-brown curl that half covered it. They were passing through the jungle. It was warm and dark and far away. Then she woke up and said, 'Have I been asleep?' and he answered, 'Yes. Are you all right? Here, let me –' And he leaned forward to . . . He bent over her. This was such bliss that he could dream no further. But it gave him the courage to bound downstairs, to snatch his straw hat from the hall, and to say as he closed the front door, 'Well, I can only try my luck, that's all.'

But his luck gave him a nasty jar, to say the least, almost immediately. Promenading up and down the garden path with Chinny and Biddy, the ancient Pekes, was the mater. Of course Reginald was fond of the mater and all that. She – she meant well, she had no end of grit, and so on. But there was no denying it, she was rather a grim parent. And there had been moments, many of them, in Reggie's life, before Uncle Alick died and left him the fruit farm, when he was convinced that to be a widow's only son was about the worst punishment a chap could have. And what made it rougher than ever was that she was positively all that he had. She wasn't only a combined parent, as it were, but she had quarrelled with all her own and the governor's relations before Reggie had won his first trouser pockets. So that whenever Reggie was homesick out there, sitting on his dark veranda by starlight, while the gramophone cried, 'Dear, what is Life but Love?' his only vision was of the mater, tall and stout, rustling down the garden path, with Chinny and Biddy at her heels . . .

The mater, with her scissors outspread to snap the head of a dead something or other, stopped at the sight of Reggie.

'You are not going out, Reginald?' she asked, seeing that he was.

'I'll be back for tea, mater,' said Reggie weakly, plunging his hands into his jacket pockets.

Snip. Off came a head. Reggie almost jumped.

'I should have thought you could have spared your mother your last afternoon,' said she.

Silence. The Pekes stared. They understood every word of the mater's. Biddy lay down with her tongue poked out; she was so fat and glossy she looked like a lump of half-melted toffee. But Chinny's porcelain eyes gloomed at Reginald, and he sniffed faintly, as though the whole world were one unpleasant smell. Snip went the scissors again. Poor little beggars; they were getting it!

'And where are you going, if your mother may ask?' asked the mater.

It was over at last, but Reggie did not slow down until he was out of sight of the house and half-way to Colonel Proctor's. Then only he noticed what a top-hole afternoon it was. It had been raining all the morning, later summer rain, warm, heavy, quick, and now the sky was clear, except for a long tail of little clouds, like ducklings, sailing over the forest. There was just enough wind to shake the last drops off the trees; one warm star splashed on his hand. Ping! – another drummed on his hat. The empty road gleamed, the hedges smelled of briar, and how big and bright the hollyhocks glowed in the cottage gardens. And here was Colonel Proctor's – here it was already. His hand was on the gate, his elbow jogged the syringa bushes and petals and pollen scattered over his coat sleeve. But wait a bit. This was too quick altogether. He'd meant to think the whole thing out again. Here, steady. But he was walking up the path, with the huge rose bushes on cither side. It can't be done like this. But his hand had grasped the bell, given it a pull, and started it pealing wildly, as if he'd come to say the house was on fire. The housemaid must have been in the hall, too, for the front door flashed open, and Reggie was shut in the empty drawing-room before that confounded bell had stopped ringing. Strangely enough, when it did, the big room, shadowy, with someone's parasol lying on top of the grand piano, bucked him up – or rather, excited him. It was so quiet, and yet in one moment the door would open, and his fate be decided. The feeling was not unlike that of being at the dentist's; he was almost reckless. But at the same time, to his immense surprise, Reggie heard himself saying, 'Lord, Thou knowest – Thou hast not done *much* for me . . .' That pulled him up; that made him realise again how dead serious it was. Too late. The door-handle turned. Anne came in, crossed the shadowy space between them, gave him her hand, and said, in her small, soft

41

voice, 'I'm so sorry, father is out. And mother is having a day in town, hat-hunting. There's only me to entertain you, Reggie.'

Reggie gasped, pressed his own hat to his jacket buttons, and stammered out, 'As a matter of fact, I've only come . . . to say good-bye.'

'Oh!' cried Anne softly – she stepped back from him and her grey eyes danced – 'what a *very* short visit!'

Then, watching him, her chin tilted, she laughed outright, a long, soft peal, and walked away from him over to the piano, and leaned against it, playing with the tassel of the parasol.

'I'm so sorry,' she said, 'to be laughing like this. I don't know why I do. It's just a bad ha-habit.' And suddenly she stamped her grey shoe, and took a pocket-handkerchief out of her white woolly jacket. 'I really must conquer it, it's too absurd,' said she.

'Good heavens, Anne,' cried Reggie, 'I love to hear you laughing! I can't imagine anything more –'

But the truth was, and they both knew it, she wasn't always laughing; it wasn't really a habit. Only ever since the day they'd met, ever since that very first moment, for some strange reason that Reggie wished to God he understood, Anne had laughed at him. Why? It didn't matter where they were or what they were talking about. They might begin by being as serious as possible, dead serious – at any rate, as far as he was concerned – but then suddenly, in the middle of a sentence, Anne would glance at him, and a little quick quiver passed over her face. Her lips parted, her eyes danced, and she began laughing.

Another queer thing about it was, Reggie had an idea she didn't herself know why she laughed. He had seen her turn away, frown, suck in her cheeks, press her hands together. But it was no use. The long, soft peal sounded, even while she cried, 'I don't know why I'm laughing.' It was a mystery . . .

Now she tucked the handkerchief away. 'Do sit down,' said she. 'And smoke, won't you? There are cigarettes in that little box beside you. I'll have one too.' He lighted a match for her, and as she bent forward he saw the tiny flame glow in the pearl ring she wore. 'It is tomorrow that you're going, isn't it?' said Anne.

'Yes, tomorrow as ever is,' said Reggie, and he blew a little fan of smoke. Why on earth was he so nervous? Nervous wasn't the word for it.

'It's – it's frightfully hard to believe,' he added.

'Yes – isn't it?' said Anne softly, and she leaned forward and rolled the point of her cigarette round the green ash-tray. How beautiful she looked like that! – simply beautiful – and she was so small in that immense chair. Reginald's heart swelled with tenderness, but it was her voice, her soft voice, that made him tremble. 'I feel you've been here for years,' she said.

Reginald took a deep breath of his cigarette. 'It's ghastly, this idea of going back,' he said.

'*Coo-roo-coo-coo-coo,*' sounded from the quiet.

'But you're fond of being out there, aren't you?' said Anne. She hooked her finger through her pearl necklace. 'Father was saying only the other night how lucky he thought you were to have a life of your

43

own.' And she looked up at him. Reginald's smile was rather wan. 'I don't feel fearfully lucky,' he said lightly.

'*Roo-coo-coo-coo*,' came again. And Anne murmured, 'You mean it's lonely.'

'Oh, it isn't the loneliness I care about,' said Reginald, and he stumped his cigarette savagely on the green ash-tray. 'I could stand any amount of it, used to like it even. It's the idea of –' Suddenly, to his horror, he felt himself blushing.

'*Roo-coo-coo-coo! Roo-coo-coo-coo!*'

Anne jumped up. 'Come and say good-bye to my doves,' she said. 'They've been moved to the side veranda. You do like doves, don't you, Reggie?'

'Awfully,' said Reggie, so fervently that as he opened the french window for her and stood to one side, Anne ran forward and laughed at the doves instead.

To and fro, to and fro over the fine red sand on the floor of the dove house, walked the two doves. One was always in front of the other. One ran forward, uttering a little cry, and the other followed, solemnly bowing and bowing. 'You see,' explained Anne, 'the one in front, she's Mrs Dove. She looks at Mr Dove and gives that little laugh and runs forward, and he follows her, bowing and bowing. And that makes her laugh again. Away she runs, and after her,' cried Anne, and she sat back on her heels, 'comes poor Mr Dove, bowing and bowing ... and that's their whole life. They never do anything else, you know.' She got up and took some yellow grains out of a bag on the roof of the dove house. 'When you think of them, out in Rhodesia, Reggie, you can be sure that is what they will be doing . . .'

Reggie gave no sign of having seen the doves or of having heard a word. For the moment he was conscious only of the immense effort it took to tear his secret out of himself and offer it to Anne. 'Anne, do you think you could ever care for me?' It was done. It was over. And in the little pause that followed Reginald saw the garden open to the light, the blue quivering sky, the flutter of leaves on the veranda poles, and Anne turning over the grains of maize on her palm with one finger. Then slowly she shut her hand, and the new world faded as she murmured slowly, 'No, never in that way.' But he had scarcely time to feel anything before she walked quickly away, and he followed her down the steps, along the garden path, under the pink rose arches, across the lawn. There, with the gay herbaceous border behind her, Anne faced Reginald. 'It isn't that I'm not awfully fond of you,' she said. 'I am. But' – her eyes widened – 'not in the way' – a quiver passed over her face – 'one ought to be fond of –' Her lips parted, and she couldn't stop herself. She began laughing. 'There, you see, you see,' she cried, 'it's your check t-tie. Even at this moment, when one would think one really would be solemn, your tie reminds me fearfully of the bow-tie that cats wear in pictures! Oh, please forgive me for being so horrid, please!'

Reggie caught hold of her little warm hand. 'There's no question of forgiving you,' he said quickly. 'How could there be? And I do believe I know why I make you laugh. It's because you're so far above me in every way that I am somehow ridiculous. I see that, Anne. But if I were to –'

'No, no.' Anne squeezed his hand hard. 'It's not that. That's all wrong. I'm not far above you at all. You're much better than I am. You're marvellously unselfish and . . . and kind and simple. I'm none of those things. You don't know me. I'm the most awful character,' said Anne. 'Please don't interrupt. And besides, that's not the point. The point is' – she shook her head – 'I couldn't possibly marry a man I laughed at. Surely you see that. The man I marry –' breathed Anne softly. She broke off. She drew her hand away, and looking at Reggie she smiled strangely, dreamily. 'The man I marry –'

And it seemed to Reggie that a tall, handsome, brilliant stranger stepped in front of him and took his place – the kind of man that Anne and he had seen often at the theatre, walking on to the stage from nowhere, without a word catching the heroine in his arms, and after one long, tremendous look, carrying her off to anywhere . . .

Reggie bowed to his vision. 'Yes, I see,' he said huskily.

'Do you?' said Anne. 'Oh, I do hope you do. Because I feel so horrid about it. It's so hard to explain. You know I've never –' She stopped. Reggie looked at her. She was smiling. 'Isn't it funny?' she said. 'I can say anything to you. I always have been able to from the very beginning.'

He tried to smile, to say 'I'm glad.' She went on. 'I've never known anyone I like as much as I like you. I've never felt so happy with anyone. But I'm sure it's not what people and what books mean when they talk about love. Do you understand? Oh, if you only knew how horrid I feel. But we'd be like . . . like Mr and Mrs Dove.'

That did it. That seemed to Reginald final, and so terribly true that he could hardly bear it. 'Don't drive it home,' he said, and he turned away from Anne and looked across the lawn. There was the gardener's cottage, with the dark ilex tree beside it. A wet, blue thumb of transparent smoke hung above the chimney. It didn't look real. How his throat ached! Could he speak? He had a shot. 'I must be getting along home,' he croaked, and he began walking across the lawn. But Anne ran after him. 'No, don't. You can't go yet,' she said imploringly. 'You can't possibly go away feeling like that.' And she stared up at him frowning, biting her lip.

'Oh, that's all right,' said Reggie, giving himself a shake. 'I'll . . . I'll –' And he waved his hand as much as to say 'get over it.'

'But this is awful,' said Anne. She clasped her hands and stood in front of him. 'Surely you do see how fatal it would be for us to marry, don't you?'

'Oh, quite, quite,' said Reggie, looking at her with haggard eyes.

'How wrong, how wicked, feeling as I do. I mean, it's all very well for Mr and Mrs Dove. But imagine that in real life – imagine it!'

47

'Oh, absolutely,' said Reggie, and he started to walk on.

But again Anne stopped him. She tugged at his sleeve, and to his astonishment, this time, instead of laughing, she looked like a little girl who was going to cry.

'Then why, if you understand, are you so un-unhappy?' she wailed. 'Why do you mind so fearfully? Why do you look so aw-awful?'

Reggie gulped, and again he waved something away. 'I can't help it,' he said, 'I've had a blow. If I cut off now, I'll be able to –'

'How can you talk of cutting off now?' said Anne scornfully. She stamped her foot at Reggie; she was crimson. 'How can you be so cruel? I can't let you go until I know for certain that you are just as happy as you were before you asked me to marry you. Surely you must see that, it's so simple.'

But it did not seem at all simple to Reginald. It seemed impossibly difficult.

'Even if I can't marry you, how can I know that you're all that way away, with only that awful mother to write to, and that you're miserable, and that it's all my fault?'

'It's not your fault. Don't think that. It's just fate.' Reggie took her hand off his sleeve and kissed it. 'Don't pity me, dear little Anne,' he said gently. And this time he nearly ran, under the pink arches, along the garden path.

'*Roo-coo-coo-coo! Roo-coo-coo-coo!*' sounded from the veranda. 'Reggie, Reggie,' from the garden.

He stopped, he turned. But when she saw his timid, puzzled look, she gave a little laugh.

'Come back, Mr Dove,' said Anne. And Reginald came slowly across the lawn.

Marriage à la Mode

On his way to the station William remembered with a fresh pang of disappointment that he was taking nothing down to the kiddies. Poor little chaps! It was hard lines on them. Their first words always were as they ran to greet him, 'What have you got for me, daddy?' and he had nothing. He would have to buy them some sweets at the station. But that was what he had done for the past four Saturdays; their faces had fallen last time when they saw the same old boxes produced again.

And Paddy had said, 'I had red ribbing on mine *bee*-fore!'

And Johnny had said, 'It's always pink on mine. I hate pink.'

But what was William to do? The affair wasn't so easily settled. In the old days, of course, he would have taken a taxi off to a decent toyshop and chosen them something in five minutes. But nowadays they had Russian toys, French toys, Serbian toys – toys from God knows where. It was over a year since Isabel had scrapped the old donkeys and engines and so on because they were so 'dreadfully sentimental' and 'so appallingly bad for the babies' sense of form.'

'It's so important,' the new Isabel had explained, 'that they should like the right things from the very beginning. It saves so much time later on. Really, if the poor pets have to spend their infant years staring at these horrors, one can imagine them growing up and asking to be taken to the Royal Academy.'

And she spoke as though a visit to the Royal Academy was certain immediate death to anyone . . .

'Well, I don't know,' said William slowly. 'When I was their age I used to go to bed hugging an old towel with a knot in it.'

The new Isabel looked at him, her eyes narrowed, her lips apart.

'*Dear* William! I'm sure you did!' She laughed in the new way.

Sweets it would have to be, however, thought William gloomily, fishing in his pocket for change for the taxi-man. And he saw the kiddies handing the boxes round – they were awfully generous little chaps – while Isabel's precious friends didn't hesitate to help themselves . . .

What about fruit? William hovered before a stall just inside the station. What about a melon each? Would they have to share that, too? Or a pineapple for Pad, and a melon for Johnny? Isabel's friends could hardly go sneaking up to the nursery at the children's meal-times. All the same, as he bought the melon William had a horrible vision of one of Isabel's young poets lapping up a slice, for some reason, behind the nursery door.

With his two very awkward parcels he strode off to his train. The platform was crowded, the train was in. Doors banged open and shut. There came such a loud hissing from the engine that people looked dazed as they scurried to and fro. William made straight for a first-class smoker, stowed away his suitcase and parcels, and taking a huge wad of papers out of his inner pocket, he flung down in the corner and began to read.

'Our client moreover is positive . . . We are inclined to reconsider . . . in the event of –' Ah, that was better. William pressed back his flattened hair and stretched his legs across the carriage floor. The familiar dull gnawing in his breast quietened down. 'With regard to our decision –' He took out a blue pencil and scored a paragraph slowly.

Two men came in, stepped across him, and made for the farther corner. A young fellow swung his golf clubs into the rack and sat down opposite. The train gave a gentle lurch, they were off. William glanced up and saw the hot, bright station slipping away. A red-faced girl raced along by the carriages, there was something strained and almost desperate in the way she waved and called. 'Hysterical!' thought William dully. Then a greasy, black-faced workman at the end of the platform grinned at the passing train. And William thought, 'A filthy life!' and went back to his papers.

When he looked up again there were fields, and beasts standing for shelter under the dark trees. A wide river, with naked children splashing in the shallows, glided into sight and was gone again. The sky shone pale, and one bird drifted high like a dark fleck in a jewel.

'We have examined our client's correspondence files . . .' The last sentence he had read echoed in his mind. 'We have examined . . .' William hung on to that sentence, but it was no good; it snapped in the middle, and the fields, the sky, the sailing bird, the water, all said, 'Isabel.' The same thing happened every Saturday afternoon. When he was on his way to meet Isabel there began those countless imaginary meetings. She was at the station, standing just a little apart from everybody else; she was sitting in the open taxi outside; she was at the garden gate; walking across the parched grass; at the door, or just inside the hall.

And her clear, light voice said, 'It's William,' or 'Hillo, William!' or 'So William has come!' He touched her cool hand, her cool cheek.

The exquisite freshness of Isabel! When he had been a little boy, it was his delight to run into the garden after a shower of rain and shake the rose-bush over him. Isabel was that rose-bush, petal-soft, sparkling and cool. And he was still that little boy. But there was no running into the garden now, no laughing and shaking. The dull, persistent gnawing in his breast started again. He drew up his legs, tossed the papers aside, and shut his eyes.

'What is it, Isabel? What is it?' he said tenderly. They were in their bedroom in the new house. Isabel sat on a painted stool before the dressing-table that was strewn with little black and green boxes.

'What is what, William?' And she bent forward, and her fine light hair fell over her cheeks.

'Ah, you know!' He stood in the middle of the strange room and he felt a stranger. At that Isabel wheeled round quickly and faced him.

'Oh, William!' she cried imploringly, and she held up the hair-brush. 'Please! Please don't be so dreadfully stuffy and – tragic. You're always saying or looking or hinting that I've changed. Just because I've got to know really congenial people, and go about more, and am frightfully keen on – on everything, you behave as though I'd' – Isabel tossed back her hair and laughed – 'killed our love or something. It's so awfully absurd' – she bit her lip – 'and it's so maddening, William. Even this new house and the servants you grudge me.'

'Isabel!'

'Yes, yes, it's true in a way,' said Isabel quickly. 'You think they are another bad sign. Oh, I know you do. I feel it,' she said softly, 'every time you come up the stairs. But we couldn't have gone on living in that other poky little hole, William. Be practical, at least! Why, there wasn't enough room for the babies even.'

No, it was true. Every morning when he came back from chambers it was to find the babies with Isabel in the back drawing-room. They were having rides on the leopard skin thrown over the sofa back, or they were playing shops with Isabel's desk for a counter, or Pad was sitting on the hearthrug rowing away for dear life with a little brass fire-shovel, while Johnny shot at pirates with the tongs. Every evening they each had a pick-a-back up the narrow stairs to their fat old Nanny.

Yes, he supposed it was a poky little house. A little white house with blue curtains and a window-box of petunias. William met their friends at the door with 'Seen our petunias? Pretty terrific for London, don't you think?'

But the imbecile thing, the absolutely extraordinary thing was that he hadn't the slightest idea that Isabel wasn't as happy as he. God, what blindness! He hadn't the remotest notion in those days that she really hated that inconvenient little house, that she thought the fat Nanny was ruining the babies, that she was desperately lonely, pining for new people and new music and pictures and so on. If they hadn't gone to that studio party at Moira Morrison's – if Moira Morrison hadn't said as they were leaving, 'I'm going to rescue your wife, selfish man. She's like an exquisite little Titania' – if Isabel hadn't gone with Moira to Paris – if – if . . .

The train stopped at another station. Bettingford. Good heavens! They'd be there in ten minutes. William stuffed the papers back into his pockets; the young man opposite had long since disappeared. Now the other two got out. The late afternoon sun shone on women in cotton frocks and little sunburnt, barefoot children. It blazed on a silky yellow flower with coarse leaves which sprawled over a bank of rock. The air ruffling through the window smelled of the sea. Had Isabel the same crowd with her this week-end, wondered William?

And he remembered the holidays they used to have, the four of them, with a little farm girl, Rose, to look after the babies. Isabel wore a jersey and her hair in a plait; she looked about fourteen. Lord! how his nose used to peel! And the amount they ate, and the amount they slept in that immense feather bed with their feet locked together . . . William couldn't help a grim smile as he thought of Isabel's horror if she knew the full extent of his sentimentality.

'Hillo, William!' She was at the station after all, standing just as he had imagined, apart from the others, and – William's heart leapt – she was alone.

'Hallo, Isabel!' William stared. He thought she looked so beautiful that he had to say something, 'You look very cool.'

'Do I?' said Isabel. 'I don't feel very cool. Come along, your horrid old train is late. The taxi's outside.' She put her hand lightly on his arm as they passed the ticket collector. 'We've all come to meet you,' she said. 'But we've left Bobby Kane at the sweet shop, to be called for.'

'Oh!' said William. It was all he could say for the moment.

There in the glare waited the taxi, with Bill Hunt and Dennis Green sprawling on one side, their hats tilted over their faces, while on the other, Moira Morrison, in a bonnet like a huge strawberry, jumped up and down.

'No ice! No ice! No ice!' she shouted gaily.

And Dennis chimed in from under his hat. '*Only* to be had from the fishmonger's.'

And Bill Hunt, emerging, added, 'With *whole* fish in it.'

'Oh, what a bore!' wailed Isabel. And she explained to William how they had been chasing round the town for ice while she waited for him. 'Simply everything is running down the steep cliffs into the sea, beginning with the butter.'

'We shall have to anoint ourselves with the butter,' said Dennis. 'May thy head, William, lack not ointment.'

'Look here,' said William, 'how are we going to sit? I'd better get up by the driver.'

'No, Bobby Kane's by the driver,' said Isabel. 'You're to sit between Moira and me.' The taxi started. 'What have you got in those mysterious parcels?'

'De-cap-it-ated heads!' said Bill Hunt, shuddering beneath his hat.

'Oh, fruit!' Isabel sounded very pleased. 'Wise William! A melon and a pineapple. How too nice!'

'No, wait a bit,' said William, smiling. But he really was anxious. 'I brought them down for the kiddies.'

'Oh, my dear!' Isabel laughed, and slipped her hand through his arm. 'They'd be rolling in agonies if they were to eat them. No' – she patted his hand – 'you must bring them something next time. I refuse to part with my pineapple.'

'Cruel Isabel! Do let me smell it!' said Moira. She flung her arms across William appealingly. 'Oh!' The strawberry bonnet fell forward: she sounded quite faint.

'A Lady in Love with a Pineapple,' said Dennis, as the taxi drew up before a little shop with a striped blind. Out came Bobby Kane, his arms full of little packets.

'I do hope they'll be good. I've chosen them because of the colours. There are some round things which really look too divine. And just look at this nougat,' he cried ecstatically, 'just look at it! It's a perfect little ballet!'

But at that moment the shopman appeared. 'Oh, I forgot. They're none of them paid for,' said Bobby, looking frightened. Isabel gave the shopman a note, and Bobby was radiant again. 'Hallo, William! I'm sitting by the driver.' And bare-headed, all in white, with his sleeves rolled up to the shoulders, he leapt into his place. 'Avanti!' he cried . . .

After tea the others went off to bathe, while William stayed and made his peace with the kiddies. But Johnny and Paddy were asleep, the rose-red glow had paled, bats were flying, and still the bathers had not returned. As William wandered downstairs, the maid crossed the hall carrying a lamp. He followed her into the sitting-room. It was a long room, coloured yellow. On the wall opposite William someone had painted a young man, over life-size, with very wobbly legs, offering a wide-eyed daisy to a young woman who had one very short arm and one very long, thin one. Over the chairs and sofa there hung strips of black material, covered with big splashes like broken eggs, and everywhere one looked there seemed to be an ash-tray full of cigarette ends. William sat down in one of the arm-chairs. Nowadays, when one felt with one hand down the sides, it wasn't to come upon a sheep with three legs or a cow that had lost one horn, or a very fat dove out of the Noah's Ark. One fished up yet another little paper-covered book of smudged-looking poems . . . He thought of the wad of papers in his pocket, but he was too hungry and tired to read. The door was open; sounds came from the kitchen. The servants were talking as if they were alone in the house. Suddenly there came a loud screech of laughter and an equally loud 'Sh!' They had remembered him. William got up and went through the french windows into the garden, and as he stood there in the shadow he heard the bathers coming up the sandy road; their voices rang through the quiet.

'I think it's up to Moira to use her little arts and wiles.'

A tragic moan from Moira.

'We ought to have a gramophone for the week-ends that played "The Maid of the Mountains."'

'Oh no! Oh no!' cried Isabel's voice. 'That's not fair to William. Be nice to him, my children! He's only staying until tomorrow evening.'

'Leave him to me,' cried Bobby Kane. 'I'm awfully good at looking after people.'

The gate swung open and shut. William moved on the terrace; they had seen him. 'Hallo, William!' And Bobby Kane, flapping his towel, began to leap and pirouette on the parched lawn. 'Pity you didn't come, William. The water was divine. And we all went to a little pub afterwards and had sloe gin.'

The others had reached the house. 'I say, Isabel,' called Bobby, 'would you like me to wear my Nijinsky dress tonight?'

'No,' said Isabel, 'nobody's going to dress. We're all starving. William's starving, too. Come along, *mes amis*, let's begin with sardines.'

'I've found the sardines,' said Moira, and she ran into the hall, holding a box high in the air.

'A Lady with a Box of Sardines,' said Dennis gravely.

'Well, William, and how's London?' asked Bill Hunt, drawing the cork out of a bottle of whisky.

'Oh, London's not much changed,' answered William.

'Good old London,' said Bobby, very hearty, spearing a sardine.

But a moment later William was forgotten. Moira Morrison began wondering what colour one's legs really were under water.

'Mine are the palest, palest mushroom colour.'

Bill and Dennis ate enormously. And Isabel filled glasses, and changed plates, and found matches, smiling blissfully. At one moment she said, 'I do wish, Bill, you'd paint it.'

'Paint what?' said Bill loudly, stuffing his mouth with bread.

'Us,' said Isabel, 'round the table. It would be so fascinating in twenty years' time.'

Bill screwed up his eyes and chewed. 'Light's wrong,' he said rudely, 'far too much yellow'; and went on eating. And that seemed to charm Isabel, too.

But after supper they were all so tired they could do nothing but yawn until it was late enough to go to bed . . .

It was not until William was waiting for his taxi the next afternoon that he found himself alone with Isabel. When he brought his suitcase down into the hall, Isabel left the others and went over to him. She stooped down and picked up the suitcase. 'What a weight!' she said, and she gave a little awkward laugh. 'Let me carry it! To the gate.'

'No, why should you?' said William. 'Of course not. Give it to me.'

'Oh, please do let me,' said Isabel. 'I want to, really.' They walked together silently. William felt there was nothing to say now.

'There,' said Isabel triumphantly, setting the suitcase down, and she looked anxiously along the sandy road. 'I hardly seem to have seen you this time,' she said breathlessly. 'It's so short, isn't it? I feel you've only just come. Next time –' The taxi came into sight. 'I hope they look after you properly in London. I'm so sorry the babies have been out all day, but Miss Neil had arranged it. They'll hate missing you. Poor William, going back to London.' The taxi turned. 'Goodbye!' She gave him a little hurried kiss; she was gone.

Fields, trees, hedges streamed by. They shook through the empty, blind-looking little town, ground up the steep pull to the station. The train was in. William made straight for a first-class smoker, flung back into the corner, but this time he let the papers alone. He folded his arms against the dull, persistent gnawing, and began in his mind to write a letter to Isabel.

The post was late as usual. They sat outside the house in long chairs under coloured parasols. Only Bobby Kane lay on the turf at Isabel's feet. It was dull, stifling; the day drooped like a flag.

'Do you think there will be Mondays in heaven?' asked Bobby childishly.

And Dennis murmured, 'Heaven will be one long Monday.'

But Isabel couldn't help wondering what had happened to the salmon they had for supper last night. She had meant to have fish mayonnaise for lunch, and now . . .

Moira was asleep. Sleeping was her latest discovery. 'It's *so* wonderful. One simply shuts one's eyes, that's all. It's *so* delicious.'

When the old ruddy postman came beating along the sandy road on his tricycle one felt the handle-bars ought to have been oars.

Bill Hunt put down his book. 'Letters,' he said complacently, and they all waited. But, heartless postman – O malignant world! There was only one, a fat one for Isabel. Not even a paper.

'And mine's only from William,' said Isabel mournfully.

'From William – already?'

'He's sending you back your marriage lines as a gentle reminder.'

'Does everybody have marriage lines? I thought they were only for servants.'

'Pages and pages! Look at her! A Lady reading a Letter,' said Dennis.

My darling, precious Isabel. Pages and pages there were. As Isabel read on her feeling of astonishment changed to a stifled feeling. What on earth had induced William . . . ? How extraordinary it was . . . What could have made him . . . ? She felt confused, more and more excited, even frightened. It was just like William. Was it? It was absurd, of course, it must be absurd, ridiculous. 'Ha, ha, ha! Oh dear!' What was she to do? Isabel flung back in her chair and laughed till she couldn't stop laughing.

'Do, do tell us,' said the others. 'You must tell us.'

'I'm longing to,' gurgled Isabel. She sat up, gathered the letter, and waved it at them. 'Gather round,' she said. 'Listen, it's too marvellous. A love-letter!'

'A love-letter! But how divine!' *Darling, precious Isabel.* But she had hardly begun before their laughter interrupted her.

'Go on, Isabel, it's perfect.'

'It's the most marvellous find.'

'Oh, do go on, Isabel!'

God forbid, my darling, that I should be a drag on your happiness.

'Oh! oh! oh!'

'Sh! sh! sh!'

And Isabel went on. When she reached the end they were hysterical: Bobby rolled on the turf and almost sobbed.

'You must let me have it just as it is, entire, for my new book,' said Dennis firmly. 'I shall give it a whole chapter.'

'Oh, Isabel,' moaned Moira, 'that wonderful bit about holding you in his arms!'

'I always thought those letters in divorce cases were made up. But they pale before this.'

'Let me hold it. Let me read it, mine own self,' said Bobby Kane.

But, to their surprise, Isabel crushed the letter in her hand. She was laughing no longer. She glanced quickly at them all; she looked exhausted. 'No, not just now. Not just now,' she stammered.

And before they could recover she had run into the house, through the hall, up the stairs into her bedroom. Down she sat on the side of the bed. 'How vile, odious, abominable, vulgar,' muttered Isabel. She pressed her eyes with her knuckles and rocked to and fro. And again she saw them, but not four, more like forty, laughing, sneering, jeering, stretching out their hands while she read them William's letter. Oh, what a loathsome thing to have done. How could she have done it! *God forbid, my darling, that I should be a drag on your happiness.* William! Isabel pressed her face into the pillow. But she felt that even the grave bedroom knew her for what she was, shallow, tinkling, vain . . .

Presently from the garden below there came voices.

'Isabel, we're all going for a bathe. Do come!'

'Come, thou wife of William!'

'Call her once before you go, call once yet!'

Isabel sat up. Now was the moment, now she must decide. Would she go with them, or stay here and write to William. Which, which should it be? 'I must make up my mind.' Oh, but how could there be any question? Of course she would stay here and write.

'Titania!' piped Moira.

'Isa-bel?'

No, it was too difficult. 'I'll – I'll go with them, and write to William later. Some other time. Later.

Not now. But I shall *certainly* write,' thought Isabel hurriedly.

And, laughing in the new way, she ran down the stairs.

Bliss

Although Bertha Young was thirty she still had moments like this when she wanted to run instead of walk, to take dancing steps on and off the pavement, to bowl a hoop, to throw something up in the air and catch it again, or to stand still and laugh at – nothing – at nothing, simply.

What can you do if you are thirty and, turning the corner of your own street, you are overcome, suddenly, by a feeling of bliss – absolute bliss! – as though you'd suddenly swallowed a bright piece of that late afternoon sun and it burned in your bosom, sending out a little shower of sparks into every particle, into every finger and toe? . . .

Oh, is there no way you can express it without being 'drunk and disorderly'? How idiotic civilisation is! Why be given a body if you have to keep it shut up in a case like a rare, rare fiddle?

'No, that about the fiddle is not quite what I mean,' she thought, running up the steps and feeling in her bag for the key – she'd forgotten it, as usual – and rattling the letter-box. 'It's not what I mean, because – Thank you, Mary' – she went into the hall. 'Is nurse back?'

'Yes, M'm.'

'And has the fruit come?'

'Yes, M'm. Everything's come.'

'Bring the fruit up to the dining-room, will you? I'll arrange it before I go upstairs.'

It was dusky in the dining-room and quite chilly. But all the same Bertha threw off her coat; she could not bear the tight clasp of it another moment, and the cold air fell on her arms.

But in her bosom there was still that bright glowing place – that shower of little sparks coming from it. It was almost unbearable. She hardly dared to breathe for fear of fanning it higher, and yet she breathed deeply, deeply. She hardly dared to look into the cold mirror – but she did look, and it gave her back a woman, radiant, with smiling, trembling lips, with big, dark eyes and an air of listening, waiting for something . . . divine to happen . . . that she knew must happen . . . infallibly.

Mary brought in the fruit on a tray and with it a glass bowl, and a blue dish, very lovely, with a strange sheen on it as though it had been dipped in milk.

'Shall I turn on the light, M'm?'

'No, thank you. I can see quite well.'

There were tangerines and apples stained with strawberry pink. Some yellow pears, smooth as silk, some white grapes covered with a silver bloom and a big cluster of purple ones. These last she had bought to tone in with the new dining-room carpet. Yes, that did sound rather far-fetched and absurd, but it was really why she had bought them. She had thought in the shop: 'I must have some purple ones to bring the carpet up to the table.' And it had seemed quite sense at the time.

When she had finished with them and had made two pyramids of these bright round shapes, she stood away from the table to get the effect – and it really was most curious. For the dark table seemed to melt into the dusky light and the glass dish and the blue bowl to float in the air. This, of course, in her present mood, was so incredibly beautiful . . . She began to laugh.

'No, no. I'm getting hysterical.' And she seized her bag and coat and ran upstairs to the nursery.

Nurse sat at a low table giving Little B her supper after her bath. The baby had on a white flannel gown and a blue woollen jacket, and her dark, fine hair was brushed up into a funny little peak. She looked up when she saw her mother and began to jump.

'Now, my lovey, eat it up like a good girl,' said nurse, setting her lips in a way that Bertha knew, and that meant she had come into the nursery at another wrong moment.

'Has she been good, Nanny?'

'She's been a little sweet all the afternoon,' whispered Nanny. 'We went to the park and I sat down on a chair and took her out of the pram and a big dog came along and put its head on my knee and she clutched its ear, tugged it. Oh, you should have seen her.'

Bertha wanted to ask if it wasn't rather dangerous to let her clutch at a strange dog's ear. But she did not dare to. She stood watching them, her hands by her side, like the poor little girl in front of the rich little girl with the doll.

The baby looked up at her again, stared, and then smiled so charmingly that Bertha couldn't help crying:

'Oh, Nanny, do let me finish giving her her supper while you put the bath things away.'

'Well, M'm, she oughtn't to be changed hands while she's eating,' said Nanny, still whispering. 'It unsettles her; it's very likely to upset her.'

How absurd it was. Why have a baby if it has to be kept – not in a case like a rare, rare, fiddle – but in another woman's arms?

'Oh, I must!' said she.

Very offended, Nanny handed her over.

'Now, don't excite her after her supper. You know you do, M'm. And I have such a time with her after!'

Thank heaven! Nanny went out of the room with the bath towels.

'Now I've got you to myself, my little precious,' said Bertha, as the baby leaned against her.

She ate delightfully, holding up her lips for the spoon and then waving her hands. Sometimes she wouldn't let the spoon go; and sometimes, just as Bertha had filled it, she waved it away to the four winds.

When the soup was finished Bertha turned round to the fire.

'You're nice – you're very nice!' said she, kissing her warm baby. 'I'm fond of you. I like you.'

And, indeed, she loved Little B so much – her neck as she bent forward, her exquisite toes as they shone transparent in the firelight – that all her feeling of bliss came back again, and again she didn't know how to express it – what to do with it.

'You're wanted on the telephone,' said Nanny, coming back in triumph and seizing *her* Little B.

Down she flew. It was Harry.

'Oh, is that you, Ber? Look here. I'll be late. I'll take a taxi and come along as quickly as I can, but get dinner put back ten minutes – will you? All right?'

'Yes, perfectly. Oh, Harry!'

'Yes?'

What had she to say? She'd nothing to say. She only wanted to get in touch with him for a moment. She couldn't absurdly cry: 'Hasn't it been a divine day!'

'What is it?' rapped out the little voice.

'Nothing. *Entendu*,' said Bertha, and hung up the receiver, thinking how much more than idiotic civilisation was.

They had people coming to dinner. The Norman Knights – a very sound couple – he was about to start a theatre, and she was awfully keen on interior decoration, a young man, Eddie Warren, who had just published a little book of poems and whom everybody was asking to dine, and a 'find' of Bertha's called Pearl Fulton. What Miss Fulton did, Bertha didn't know. They had met at the club and Bertha had fallen in love with her, as she always did fall in love with beautiful women who had something strange about them.

The provoking thing was that, though they had been about together and met a number of times and really talked, Bertha couldn't make her out. Up to a certain point Miss Fulton was rarely, wonderfully frank, but the certain point was there, and beyond that she would not go.

Was there anything beyond it? Harry said 'No.' Voted her dullish, and 'cold like all blonde women, with a touch, perhaps, of anæmia of the brain.' But Bertha wouldn't agree with him; not yet, at any rate.

'No, the way she has of sitting with her head a little on one side, and smiling, has something behind it, Harry, and I must find out what that something is.'

'Most likely it's a good stomach,' answered Harry.

He made a point of catching Bertha's heels with replies of that kind . . . 'liver frozen, my dear girl,' or 'pure flatulence,' or 'kidney disease,' . . . and so on. For some strange reason Bertha liked this, and almost admired it in him very much.

She went into the drawing-room and lighted the fire; then, picking up the cushions, one by one, that Mary had disposed so carefully, she threw them back on to the chairs and the couches. That made all the difference; the room came alive at once. As she was about to throw the last one she surprised herself by suddenly hugging it to her, passionately, passionately. But it did not put out the fire in her bosom. Oh, on the contrary!

The windows of the drawing-room opened on to a balcony overlooking the garden. At the far end, against the wall, there was a tall, slender pear tree in fullest, richest bloom; it stood perfect, as though becalmed against the jade-green sky. Bertha couldn't help feeling, even from this distance, that it had not a single bud or a faded petal. Down below, in the garden beds, the red and yellow tulips, heavy with flowers, seemed to lean upon the dusk. A grey cat, dragging its belly, crept across the lawn, and a black one, its shadow, trailed after. The sight of them, so intent and so quick, gave Bertha a curious shiver.

'What creepy things cats are!' she stammered, and she turned away from the window and began walking up and down . . .

How strong the jonquils smelled in the warm room. Too strong? Oh, no. And yet, as though overcome, she flung down on a couch and pressed her hands to her eyes.

'I'm too happy – too happy!' she murmured.

And she seemed to see on her eyelids the lovely pear tree with its wide open blossoms as a symbol of her own life.

Really – really – she had everything. She was young. Harry and she were as much in love as ever, and they got on together splendidly and were really good pals. She had an adorable baby. They didn't have to worry about money. They had this absolutely satisfactory house and garden. And friends – modern, thrilling friends, writers and painters and poets or people keen on social questions – just the kind of friends they wanted. And then there were books, and there was music, and she had found a wonderful little dressmaker, and they were going abroad in the summer, and their new cook made the most superb omelettes . . .

'I'm absurd. Absurd!' She sat up; but she felt quite dizzy, quite drunk. It must have been the spring.

Yes, it was the spring. Now she was so tired she could not drag herself upstairs to dress.

A white dress, a string of jade beads, green shoes and stockings. It wasn't intentional. She had thought of this scheme hours before she stood at the drawing-room window.

Her petals rustled softly into the hall, and she kissed Mrs Norman Knight, who was taking off the most amusing orange coat with a procession of black monkeys round the hem and up the fronts.

'. . . Why! Why! Why is the middle-class so stodgy – so utterly without a sense of humour! My dear, it's only by a fluke that I am here at all – Norman being the protective fluke. For my darling monkeys so upset the train that it rose to a man and simply ate me with its eyes. Didn't laugh – wasn't amused – that I should have loved. No, just stared – and bored me through and through.'

'But the cream of it was,' said Norman, pressing a large tortoiseshell-rimmed monocle into his eye, 'you don't mind me telling this, Face, do you?' (In their home and among their friends they called each other Face and Mug.) 'The cream of it was when she, being full fed, turned to the woman beside her and said: "Haven't you ever seen a monkey before?"'

'Oh yes!' Mrs Norman Knight joined in the laughter. 'Wasn't that too absolutely creamy?'

And a funnier thing still was that now her coat was off she did look like a very intelligent monkey – who had even made that yellow silk dress out of scraped banana skins. And her amber ear-rings: they were like little dangling nuts.

'This is a sad, sad fall!' said Mug, pausing in front of Little B's perambulator. 'When the perambulator comes into the hall –' and he waved the rest of the quotation away.

The bell rang. It was lean, pale Eddie Warren (as usual) in a state of acute distress.

'It *is* the right house, *isn't* it?' he pleaded.

'Oh, I think so – I hope so,' said Bertha brightly.

'I have had such a *dreadful* experience with a taxi-man; he was *most* sinister. I couldn't get him to *stop*. The *more* I knocked and called the *faster* he went. And *in* the moonlight this *bizarre* figure with the *flattened* head *crouching* over the *lit-tle* wheel . . .'

He shuddered, taking off an immense white silk scarf. Bertha noticed that his socks were white, too – most charming.

'But how dreadful!' she cried.

'Yes, it really was,' said Eddie, following her into the drawing-room. 'I saw myself *driving* through Eternity in a *timeless* taxi.'

He knew the Norman Knights. In fact, he was going to write a play for N. K. when the theatre scheme came off.

'Well, Warren, how's the play?' said Norman Knight, dropping his monocle and giving his eye a moment in which to rise to the surface before it was screwed down again.

And Mrs Norman Knight: 'Oh, Mr Warren, what happy socks?'

'I *am* so glad you like them,' said he, staring at his feet. 'They seem to have got so *much* whiter since the moon rose.' And he turned his lean sorrowful young face to Bertha. 'There *is* a moon, you know.'

She wanted to cry: 'I am sure there is – often – often!'

He really was a most attractive person. But so was Face, crouched before the fire in her banana skins, and so was Mug, smoking a cigarette and saying as he flicked the ash: 'Why doth the bridegroom tarry?'

'There he is, now.'

Bang went the front door open and shut. Harry shouted: 'Hullo, you people. Down in five minutes.' And they heard him swarm up the stairs. Bertha couldn't help smiling; she knew how he loved doing things at high pressure. What, after all, did an extra five minutes matter? But he would pretend to himself that they mattered beyond measure. And then he would make a great point of coming into the drawing-room, extravagantly cool and collected.

Harry had such a zest for life. Oh, how she appreciated it in him. And his passion for fighting – for seeking in everything that came up against him another test of his power and of his courage – that, too, she understood. Even when it made him just occasionally, to other people, who didn't know him well, a little ridiculous perhaps . . . For there were moments when he rushed into battle where no battle was . . . She talked and laughed and positively forgot until he had come in (just as she had imagined) that Pearl Fulton had not turned up.

'I wonder if Miss Fulton has forgotten?'

'I expect so,' said Harry. 'Is she on the 'phone?'

'Ah! There's a taxi now.' And Bertha smiled with that little air of proprietorship that she always assumed while her women finds were new and mysterious. 'She lives in taxis.'

'She'll run to fat if she does,' said Harry coolly, ringing the bell for dinner. 'Frightful danger for blonde women.'

'Harry – don't,' warned Bertha, laughing up at him.

Came another tiny moment, while they waited, laughing and talking, just a trifle too much at their ease, a trifle too unaware. And then Miss Fulton, all in silver, with a silver fillet binding her pale blonde hair, came in smiling, her head a little on one side.

'Am I late?'

'No, not at all,' said Bertha. 'Come along.' And she took her arm and they moved into the dining-room.

What was there in the touch of that cool arm that could fan – fan – start blazing – blazing – the fire of bliss that Bertha did not know what to do with?

Miss Fulton did not look at her; but then she seldom did look at people directly. Her heavy eyelids lay upon her eyes and the strange half-smile came and went upon her lips as though she lived by listening rather than seeing. But Bertha knew, suddenly, as if the longest, most intimate look had passed between them – as if they had said to each other: 'You, too?' – that Pearl Fulton, stirring the beautiful red soup in the grey plate, was feeling just what she was feeling.

And the others? Face and Mug, Eddie and Harry,

their spoons rising and falling – dabbing their lips with their napkins, crumbling bread, fiddling with the forks and glasses and talking.

'I met her at the Alpha show – the weirdest little person. She'd not only cut off her hair, but she seemed to have taken a dreadfully good snip off her legs and arms and her neck and her poor little nose as well.'

'Isn't she very *liée* with Michael Oat?'

'The man who wrote *Love in False Teeth*?'

'He wants to write a play for me. One act. One man. Decides to commit suicide. Gives all the reasons why he should and why he shouldn't. And just as he has made up his mind either to do it or not to do it – curtain. Not half a bad idea.'

'What's he going to call it – "Stomach Trouble"?'

'I *think* I've come across the *same* idea in a lit-tle French review, *quite* unknown in England.'

No, they didn't share it. They were dears – dears – and she loved having them there, at her table, and giving them delicious food and wine. In fact, she longed to tell them how delightful they were, and what a decorative group they made, how they seemed to set one another off and how they reminded her of a play by Tchekof!

Harry was enjoying his dinner. It was part of his – well, not his nature, exactly, and certainly not his pose – his – something or other – to talk about food and to glory in his 'shameless passion for the white flesh of the lobster' and 'the green of pistachio ices – green and cold like the eyelids of Egyptian dancers.'

When he looked up at her and said: 'Bertha, this is

a very admirable *soufflé*!' she almost could have wept with child-like pleasure.

Oh, why did she feel so tender towards the whole world tonight? Everything was good – was right. All that happened seemed to fill again her brimming cup of bliss.

And still, in the back of her mind, there was the pear tree. It would be silver now, in the light of poor dear Eddie's moon, silver as Miss Fulton, who sat there turning a tangerine in her slender fingers that were so pale a light seemed to come from them.

What she simply couldn't make out – what was miraculous – was how she should have guessed Miss Fulton's mood so exactly and so instantly. For she never doubted for a moment that she was right, and yet what had she to go on? Less than nothing.

'I believe this does happen very, very rarely between women. Never between men,' thought Bertha. 'But while I am making the coffee in the drawing-room perhaps she will "give a sign."'

What she meant by that she did not know, and what would happen after that she could not imagine.

While she thought like this she saw herself talking and laughing. She had to talk because of her desire to laugh.

'I must laugh or die.'

But when she noticed Face's funny little habit of tucking something down the front of her bodice – as if she kept a tiny, secret hoard of nuts there, too – Bertha had to dig her nails into her hands – so as not to laugh too much.

*

It was over at last. And: 'Come and see my new coffee machine,' said Bertha.

'We only have a new coffee machine once a fort-night,' said Harry. Face took her arm this time; Miss Fulton bent her head and followed after.

The fire had died down in the drawing-room to a red, flickering 'nest of baby phœnixes,' said Face.

'Don't turn up the light for a moment. It is so lovely.' And down she crouched by the fire again. She was always cold . . . 'without her little red flannel jacket, of course,' thought Bertha.

At that moment Miss Fulton 'gave the sign.'

'Have you a garden?' said the cool, sleepy voice.

This was so exquisite on her part that all Bertha could do was to obey. She crossed the room, pulled the curtains apart, and opened those long windows.

'There!' she breathed.

And the two women stood side by side looking at the slender, flowering tree. Although it was so still it seemed, like the flame of a candle, to stretch up, to point, to quiver in the bright air, to grow taller and taller as they gazed – almost to touch the rim of the round, silver moon.

How long did they stand there? Both, as it were, caught in that circle of unearthly light, understanding each other perfectly, creatures of another world, and wondering what they were to do in this one with all this blissful treasure that burned in their bosoms and dropped, in silver flowers, from their hair and hands?

For ever – for a moment? And did Miss Fulton murmur: 'Yes. Just *that*.' Or did Bertha dream it?

Then the light was snapped on and Face made the coffee and Harry said: 'My dear Mrs Knight, don't ask me about my baby. I never see her. I shan't feel the slightest interest in her until she has a lover,' and Mug took his eye out of the conservatory for a moment and then put it under glass again and Eddie Warren drank his coffee and set down the cup with a face of anguish as though he had drunk and seen the spider.

'What I want to do is to give the young men a show. I believe London is simply teeming with first-chop, unwritten plays. What I want to say to 'em is: "Here's the theatre. Fire ahead."'

'You know, my dear, I am going to decorate a room for the Jacob Nathans. Oh, I am so tempted to do a fried-fish scheme, with the backs of the chairs shaped like frying-pans and lovely chip potatoes embroidered all over the curtains.'

'The trouble with our young writing men is that they are still too romantic. You can't put out to sea without being seasick and wanting a basin. Well, why won't they have the courage of those basins?'

'A *dreadful* poem about a *girl* who was *violated* by a beggar *without* a nose in a lit-tle wood . . .'

Miss Fulton sank into the lowest, deepest chair and Harry handed round the cigarettes.

From the way he stood in front of her shaking the silver box and saying abruptly: 'Egyptian? Turkish? Virginian? They're all mixed up,' Bertha realised that she not only bored him; he really disliked her. And she decided from the way Miss Fulton said: 'No, thank you, I won't smoke,' that she felt it, too, and was hurt.

'Oh, Harry, don't dislike her. You are quite wrong about her. She's wonderful, wonderful. And, besides, how can you feel so differently about someone who means so much to me. I shall try to tell you when we are in bed tonight what has been happening. What she and I have shared.'

At those last words something strange and almost terrifying darted into Bertha's mind. And this something blind and smiling whispered to her: 'Soon these people will go. The house will be quiet – quiet. The lights will be out. And you and he will be alone together in the dark room – the warm bed . . .'

She jumped up from her chair and ran over to the piano.

'What a pity someone does not play!' she cried. 'What a pity somebody does not play.'

For the first time in her life Bertha Young desired her husband.

Oh, she'd loved him – she'd been in love with him, of course, in every other way, but just not in that way. And equally, of course, she'd understood that he was different. They'd discussed it so often. It had worried her dreadfully at first to find that she was so cold, but after a time it had not seemed to matter. They were so frank with each other – such good pals. That was the best of being modern.

But now – ardently! ardently! The word ached in her ardent body! Was this what that feeling of bliss had been leading up to? But then, then –

'My dear,' said Mrs Norman Knight, 'you know our

shame. We are the victims of time and train. We live in Hampstead. It's been so nice.'

'I'll come with you into the hall,' said Bertha. 'I loved having you. But you must not miss the last train. That's so awful, isn't it?'

'Have a whisky, Knight, before you go?' called Harry.

'No, thanks, old chap.'

Bertha squeezed his hand for that as she shook it.

'Good night, goodbye,' she cried from the top step, feeling that this self of hers was taking leave of them for ever.

When she got back into the drawing-room the others were on the move.

'. . . Then you can come part of the way in my taxi.'

'I shall be *so* thankful *not* to have to face *another* drive *alone* after my *dreadful* experience.'

'You can get a taxi at the rank just at the end of the street. You won't have to walk more than a few yards.'

'That's a comfort. I'll go and put on my coat.'

Miss Fulton moved towards the hall and Bertha was following when Harry almost pushed past.

'Let me help you.'

Bertha knew that he was repenting his rudeness – she let him go. What a boy he was in some ways – so impulsive – so – simple.

And Eddie and she were left by the fire.

'I *wonder* if you have seen Bilks' *new* poem called *Table d'Hôte*,' said Eddie softly. 'It's *so* wonderful. In the last Anthology. Have you got a copy? I'd *so* like to *show* it to you. It begins with an *incredibly* beautiful line: "Why Must it Always be Tomato Soup?"'

'Yes,' said Bertha. And she moved noiselessly to a table opposite the drawing-room door and Eddie glided noiselessly after her. She picked up the little book and gave it to him; they had not made a sound.

While he looked it up she turned her head towards the hall. And she saw ... Harry with Miss Fulton's coat in his arms and Miss Fulton with her back turned to him and her head bent. He tossed the coat away, put his hands on her shoulders and turned her violently to him. His lips said: 'I adore you,' and Miss Fulton laid her moonbeam fingers on his cheeks and smiled her sleepy smile. Harry's nostrils quivered; his lips curled back in a hideous grin while he whispered: 'Tomorrow,' and with her eyelids Miss Fulton said: 'Yes.'

'Here it is,' said Eddie. '"Why Must it Always be Tomato Soup?" It's so *deeply* true, don't you feel? Tomato soup is so *dreadfully* eternal.'

'If you prefer,' said Harry's voice, very loud, from the hall, 'I can 'phone you a cab to come to the door.'

'Oh, no. It's not necessary,' said Miss Fulton, and she came up to Bertha and gave her the slender fingers to hold.

'Goodbye. Thank you so much.'

'Goodbye,' said Bertha.

Miss Fulton held her hand a moment longer.

'Your lovely pear tree!' she murmured.

And then she was gone, with Eddie following, like the black cat following the grey cat.

'I'll shut up shop,' said Harry, extravagantly cool and collected.

'Your lovely pear tree – pear tree – pear tree!'

Bertha simply ran over to the long windows.

'Oh, what is going to happen now?' she cried.

But the pear tree was as lovely as ever and as full of flower and as still.

Honeymoon

And when they came out of the lace shop there was their own driver and the cab they called their own cab waiting for them under a plane tree. What luck! Wasn't it luck? Fanny pressed her husband's arm. These things seemed always to be happening to them ever since they – came abroad. Didn't he think so too? But George stood on the pavement edge, lifted his stick, and gave a loud 'Hi!' Fanny sometimes felt a little uncomfortable about the way George summoned cabs, but the drivers didn't seem to mind, so it must have been all right. Fat, good-natured, and smiling, they stuffed away the little newspaper they were reading, whipped the cotton cover off the horse, and were ready to obey.

'I say,' George said as he helped Fanny in, 'suppose we go and have tea at the place where the lobsters grow. Would you like to?'

'Most awfully,' said Fanny fervently, as she leaned back wondering why the way George put things made them sound so very nice.

'R-right, *bien*.' He was beside her. '*Allay*,' he cried gaily, and off they went.

Off they went, spanking along lightly, under the green and gold shade of the plane trees, through the small streets that smelled of lemons and fresh coffee, past the fountain square where women, with water-pots

85

lifted, stopped talking to gaze after them, round the corner past the café, with its pink and white umbrellas, green tables, and blue siphons, and so to the sea front. There a wind, light, warm, came flowing over the boundless sea. It touched George, and Fanny it seemed to linger over while they gazed at the dazzling water. And George said, 'Jolly, isn't it?' And Fanny, looking dreamy, said, as she said at least twenty times a day since they – came abroad: 'Isn't it extraordinary to think that here we are quite alone, away from everybody, with nobody to tell us to go home, or to – to order us about except ourselves?'

George had long since given up answering 'Extraordinary!' As a rule he merely kissed her. But now he caught hold of her hand, stuffed it into his pocket, pressed her fingers, and said, 'I used to keep a white mouse in my pocket when I was a kid.'

'Did you?' said Fanny, who was intensely interested in everything George had ever done. 'Were you very fond of white mice?'

'Fairly,' said George, without conviction. He was looking at something, bobbing out there beyond the bathing steps. Suddenly he almost jumped in his seat. 'Fanny!' he cried. 'There's a chap out there bathing. Do you see? I'd no idea people had begun. I've been missing it all these days.' George glared at the reddened face, the reddened arm, as though he could not look away. 'At any rate,' he muttered, 'wild horses won't keep me from going in tomorrow morning.'

Fanny's heart sank. She had heard for years of the frightful dangers of the Mediterranean. It was an absolute death-trap. Beautiful, treacherous Mediterranean. There it lay curled before them, it's white, silky paws touching the stones and gone again . . . But she'd made up her mind long before she was married that never would she be the kind of woman who interfered with her husband's pleasures, so all she said was, airily, 'I suppose one has to be very up in the currents, doesn't one?'

'Oh, I don't know,' said George. 'People talk an awful lot of rot about the danger.'

But now they were passing a high wall on the land side, covered with flowering heliotrope, and Fanny's little nose lifted. 'Oh, George,' she breathed. 'The smell! The most divine . . .'

'Topping villa,' said George. 'Look, you can see it through the palms.'

'Isn't it rather large?' said Fanny, who somehow could not look at any villa except as a possible habitation for herself and George.

'Well, you'd need a crowd of people if you stayed there long,' replied George. 'Deadly, otherwise. I say, it is ripping. I wonder who it belongs to.' And he prodded the driver in the back.

The lazy, smiling driver, who had no idea, replied, as he always did on these occasions, that it was the property of a wealthy Spanish family.

'Masses of Spaniards on this coast,' commented George, leaning back again, and they were silent until, as they rounded a bend, the big, bone-white hotel-restaurant came into view. Before it there was a small terrace built up against the sea, planted with umbrella palms, set out with tables, and at their approach, from the terrace, from the hotel, waiters came running to receive, to welcome Fanny and George, to cut them off from any possible kind of escape.

'Outside?'

Oh, but of course they would sit outside. The sleek manager, who was marvellously like a fish in a frock-coat, skimmed forward.

'Dis way, sir. Dis way, sir. I have a very nice little table,' he gasped. 'Just the little table for you, sir, over in de corner. Dis way.'

So George, looking most dreadfully bored, and Fanny, trying to look as though she'd spent years of life threading her way through strangers, followed after.

'Here you are, sir. Here you will be very nice,' coaxed the manager, taking the vase off the table, and putting it down again as if it were a fresh little bouquet out of the air. But George refused to sit down immediately. He saw through these fellows; he wasn't going to be done. These chaps were always out to rush you. So he put his hands in his pockets, and said to Fanny, very calmly, 'This all right for you? Anywhere else you'd prefer? How about over there?' And he nodded to a table right over the other side.

What it was to be a man of the world! Fanny admired him deeply, but all she wanted to do was to sit down and look like everybody else.

'I – I like this,' said she.

'Right,' said George hastily, and he sat down almost before Fanny, and said quickly, 'Tea for two and chocolate éclairs.'

'Very good, sir,' said the manager, and his mouth opened and shut as though he was ready for another dive under the water. 'You will not 'ave toasts to start with? We 'ave very nice toasts, sir.'

'No,' said George shortly. 'You don't want toast, do you, Fanny?'

'Oh no, thank you, George,' said Fanny, praying the manager would go.

'Or perhaps de lady might like to look at de live lobsters in de tank while de tea is coming?' And he grimaced and smirked and flicked his serviette like a fin.

George's face grew stony. He said 'No' again, and Fanny bent over the table, unbuttoning her gloves. When she looked up the man was gone. George took off his hat, tossed it on to a chair, and pressed back his hair.

'Thank God,' said he, 'that chap's gone. These foreign fellows bore me stiff. The only way to get rid of them is simply to shut up as you saw I did. Thank heaven!' sighed George again, with so much emotion that if it hadn't been ridiculous Fanny might have imagined that he had been as frightened of the manager as she. As it was she felt a rush of love for George. His hands were on the table, brown, large hands that she knew so well. She longed to take one of them and squeeze it hard. But, to her astonishment, George did just that thing. Leaning across the table, he put his hand over hers, and said, without looking at her, 'Fanny, darling Fanny!'

'Oh, George!' It was in that heavenly moment that

Fanny heard a *twing-twing-tootle-tootle*, and a light strumming. There's going to be music, she thought, but the music didn't matter just then. Nothing mattered except love. Faintly smiling she gazed into that faintly smiling face, and the feeling was so blissful that she felt inclined to say to George, 'Let us stay here – where we are – at this little table. It's perfect, and the sea is perfect. Let us stay.' But instead her eyes grew serious.

'Darling,' said Fanny. 'I want to ask you something fearfully important. Promise me you'll answer. Promise.'

'I promise,' said George, too solemn to be quite as serious as she.

'It's this.' Fanny paused a moment, looked down, looked up again. 'Do you feel,' she said softly, 'that you really know me now? But really, really know *me*?'

It was too much for George. Know his Fanny? He gave a broad, childish grin. 'I should jolly well think I do,' he said emphatically. 'Why, what's up?'

Fanny felt he hadn't quite understood. She went on quickly: 'What I mean is this. So often people, even when they love each other, don't seem to – to – it's so hard to say – know each other perfectly. They don't seem to want to. And I think that's awful. They misunderstand each other about the most important things of all.' Fanny looked horrified. 'George, we couldn't do that, could we? We never could.'

'Couldn't be done,' laughed George, and he was just going to tell her how much he liked her little nose, when the waiter arrived with the tea and the band struck up. It was a flute, a guitar, and a violin, and it played so gaily that Fanny felt if she wasn't careful even the cups and saucers might grow little wings and fly away. George absorbed three chocolate éclairs, Fanny two. The funny-tasting tea – 'Lobster in the kettle,' shouted George above the music – was nice all the same, and when the tray was pushed aside and George was smoking, Fanny felt bold enough to look at the other people. But it was the band grouped under one of the dark trees that fascinated her most. The fat man stroking the guitar was like a picture. The dark man playing the flute kept raising his eyebrows as though he was astonished at the sounds that came from it. The fiddler was in shadow.

The music stopped as suddenly as it had begun. It was then she noticed a tall old man with white hair standing beside the musicians. Strange she hadn't noticed him before. He wore a very high, glazed collar, a coat green at the seams, and shamefully shabby button boots. Was he another manager? He did not look like a manager, and yet he stood there gazing over the tables as though thinking of something different and far away from all this. Who could he be?

Presently, as Fanny watched him, he touched the points of his collar with his fingers, coughed slightly, and half turned to the band. It began to play again. Something boisterous, reckless, full of fire, full of passion, was tossed into the air, was tossed to that quiet figure, which clasped its hands, and still with that far-away look, began to sing.

'Good Lord!' said George. It seemed that everybody

was equally astonished. Even the little children eating ices stared, with their spoons in the air ... Nothing was heard except a thin, faint voice, the memory of a voice singing something in Spanish. It wavered, beat on, touched the high notes, fell again, seemed to implore, to entreat, to beg for something, and then the tune changed, and it was resigned, it bowed down, it knew it was denied.

Almost before the end a little child gave a squeak of laughter, but everybody was smiling – except Fanny and George. Is life like this too? thought Fanny. There are people like this. There is suffering. And she looked at that gorgeous sea, lapping the land as though it loved it, and the sky, bright with the brightness before evening. Had she and George the right to be so happy? Wasn't it cruel? There must be something else in life which made all these things possible. What was it? She turned to George.

But George had been feeling differently from Fanny. The poor old boy's voice was funny in a way, but, God, how it made you realise what a terrific thing it was to be at the beginning of everything, as they were, he and Fanny! George, too, gazed at the bright, breathing water, and his lips opened as if he could drink it. How fine it was! There was nothing like the sea for making a chap feel fit. And there sat Fanny, his Fanny, leaning forward, breathing so gently.

'Fanny!' George called to her.

As she turned to him something in her soft, wondering look made George feel that for two pins he would jump over the table and carry her off.

'I say,' said George rapidly, 'let's go, shall we? Let's go back to the hotel. Come. Do, Fanny darling. Let's go now.'

The band began to play. 'Oh, God!' almost groaned George. 'Let's go before the old codger begins squawking again.'

And a moment later they were gone.

A Dill Pickle

And then, after six years, she saw him again. He was seated at one of those little bamboo tables decorated with a Japanese vase of paper daffodils. There was a tall plate of fruit in front of him, and very carefully, in a way she recognised immediately as his 'special' way, he was peeling an orange.

He must have felt that shock of recognition in her, for he looked up and met her eyes. Incredible! He didn't know her! She smiled; he frowned. She came towards him. He closed his eyes an instant, but opening them his face lit up as though he had struck a match in a dark room. He laid down the orange and pushed back his chair, and she took her little warm hand out of her muff and gave it to him.

'Vera!' he exclaimed. 'How strange. Really, for a moment I didn't know you. Won't you sit down? You've had lunch? Won't you have some coffee?'

She hesitated, but of course she meant to.

'Yes, I'd like some coffee.' And she sat down opposite him.

'You've changed. You've changed very much,' he said, staring at her with that eager, lighted look. 'You look so well. I've never seen you look so well before.'

'Really?' She raised her veil and unbuttoned her high

fur collar. 'I don't feel very well. I can't bear this weather, you know.'

'Ah, no. You hate the cold . . .'

'Loathe it.' She shuddered. 'And the worst of it is that the older one grows . . .'

He interrupted her. 'Excuse me,' and tapped on the table for the waitress. 'Please bring some coffee and cream.' To her: 'You are sure you won't eat anything? Some fruit, perhaps. The fruit here is very good.'

'No, thanks. Nothing.'

'Then that's settled.' And smiling just a hint too broadly he took up the orange again. 'You were saying – the older one grows –'

'The colder,' she laughed. But she was thinking how well she remembered that trick of his – the trick of interrupting her – and how it used to exasperate her six years ago. She used to feel then as though he, quite suddenly, in the middle of what she was saying, put his hand over her lips, turned from her, attended to something different, and then took his hand away, and with just the same slightly too broad smile, gave her his attention again . . . Now we are ready. That is settled.

'The colder!' He echoed her words, laughing too. 'Ah, ah. You still say the same things. And there is another thing about you that is not changed at all – your beautiful voice – your beautiful way of speaking.' Now he was very grave; he leaned towards her, and she smelled the warm, stinging scent of the orange peel. 'You have only to say one word and I would know your

95

voice among all other voices. I don't know what it is –
I've often wondered – that makes your voice such a
– haunting memory . . . Do you remember that first
afternoon we spent together at Kew Gardens? You
were so surprised because I did not know the names of
any flowers. I am still just as ignorant for all your telling
me. But whenever it is very fine and warm, and I see
some bright colours – it's awfully strange – I hear your
voice saying: 'Geranium, marigold and verbena.' And I
feel those three words are all I recall of some forgotten,
heavenly language . . . You remember that afternoon?'

'Oh, yes, very well.' She drew a long, soft breath, as
though the paper daffodils between them were almost
too sweet to bear. Yet, what had remained in her mind
of that particular afternoon was an absurd scene over
the tea-table. A great many people taking tea in a
Chinese pagoda, and he behaving like a maniac about
the wasps – waving them away, flapping at them with
his straw hat, serious and infuriated out of all pro-
portion to the occasion. How delighted the sniggering
tea drinkers had been. And how she had suffered.

But now, as he spoke, that memory faded. His was
the truer. Yes, it had been a wonderful afternoon, full
of geranium and marigold and verbena, and – warm
sunshine. Her thoughts lingered over the last two
words as though she sang them.

In the warmth, as it were, another memory unfolded.
She saw herself sitting on a lawn. He lay beside her,
and suddenly, after a long silence, he rolled over and
put his head in her lap.

'I wish,' he said, in a low, troubled voice, 'I wish that

I had taken poison and were about to die – here now!'

At that moment a little girl in a white dress, holding a long, dripping white lily, dodged from behind a bush, stared at them, and dodged back again. But he did not see. She leaned over him.

'Ah, why do you say that? I could not say that.'

But he gave a kind of soft moan, and taking her hand he held it to his cheek.

'Because I know I am going to love you too much – far too much. And I shall suffer so terribly, Vera, because you never, never will love me.'

He was certainly far better looking now than he had been then. He had lost all that dreamy vagueness and indecision. Now he had the air of a man who has found his place in life, and fills it with a confidence and an assurance which was, to say the least, impressive. He must have made money, too. His clothes were admirable, and at that moment he pulled a Russian cigarette-case out of his pocket.

'Won't you smoke?'

'Yes, I will.' She hovered over them. 'They look very good.'

'I think they are. I get them made for me by a little man in St James's Street. I don't smoke very much. I'm not like you – but when I do, they must be delicious, very fresh cigarettes. Smoking isn't a habit with me; it's a luxury – like perfume. Are you still so fond of perfumes? Ah, when I was in Russia . . .'

She broke in: 'You've really been to Russia?'

'Oh yes. I was there for over a year. Have you forgotten how we used to talk of going there?'

'No, I've not forgotten.'

He gave a strange half-laugh and leaned back in his chair. 'Isn't it curious. I have really carried out all those journeys that we planned. Yes, I have been to all those places that we talked of, and stayed in them long enough to – as you used to say – 'air oneself' in them. In fact, I have spent the last three years of my life travelling all the time. Spain, Corsica, Siberia, Russia, Egypt. The only country left is China, and I mean to go there, too, when the war is over.'

As he spoke, so lightly, tapping the end of his cigarette against the ash-tray, she felt the strange beast that had slumbered so long within her bosom stir, stretch itself, yawn, prick up its ears, and suddenly bound to its feet, and fix its longing, hungry stare upon those far-away places. But all she said was, smiling gently: 'How I envy you.'

He accepted that. 'It has been,' he said, 'very wonderful – especially Russia. Russia was all that we had imagined, and far, far more. I even spent some days on a river boat on the Volga. Do you remember that boatman's song that you used to play?'

'Yes.' It began to play in her mind as she spoke.

'Do you ever play it now?'

'No, I've no piano.'

He was amazed at that. 'But what has become of your beautiful piano?'

She made a little grimace. 'Sold. Ages ago.'

'But you were so fond of music,' he wondered.

'I've no time for it now,' said she.

He let it go at that. 'That river life,' he went on, 'is

something quite special. After a day or two you cannot realise that you have ever known another. And it is not necessary to know the language – the life of the boat creates a bond between you and the people that's more than sufficient. You eat with them, pass the day with them, and in the evening there is that endless singing.'

She shivered, hearing the boatman's song break out again loud and tragic, and seeing the boat floating on the darkening river with melancholy trees on either side . . . 'Yes, I should like that,' said she, stroking her muff.

'You'd like almost everything about Russian life,' he said warmly. 'It's so informal, so impulsive, so free without question. And then the peasants are so splendid. They are such human beings – yes, that is it. Even the man who drives your carriage has – has some real part in what is happening. I remember the evening a party of us, two friends of mine and the wife of one of them, went for a picnic by the Black Sea. We took supper and champagne and ate and drank on the grass. And while we were eating the coachman came up. "Have a dill pickle," he said. He wanted to share with us. That seemed to me so right, so – you know what I mean?'

And she seemed at that moment to be sitting on the grass beside the mysteriously Black Sea, black as velvet, and rippling against the banks in silent, velvet waves. She saw the carriage drawn up to one side of the road, and the little group on the grass, their faces and hands white in the moonlight. She saw the pale dress of the woman outspread and her folded parasol, lying on the grass like a huge pearl crochet-hook. Apart from them, with his supper in a cloth on his knees, sat the coachman. 'Have a dill pickle,' said he, and although she was not certain what a dill pickle was, she saw the greenish glass jar with a red chilli like a parrot's beak glimmering through. She sucked in her cheeks; the dill pickle was terribly sour . . .

'Yes, I know perfectly what you mean,' she said.

In the pause that followed they looked at each other. In the past when they had looked at each other like that they had felt such a boundless understanding between them that their souls had, as it were, put their arms round each other and dropped into the same sea, content to be drowned, like mournful lovers. But now, the surprising thing was that it was he who held back. He who said:

'What a marvellous listener you are. When you look at me with those wild eyes I feel that I could tell you things that I would never breathe to another human being.'

Was there just a hint of mockery in his voice or was it her fancy? She could not be sure.

'Before I met you,' he said, 'I had never spoken of myself to anybody. How well I remember one night, the night that I brought you the little Christmas tree, telling you all about my childhood. And of how I was so miserable that I ran away and lived under a cart in our yard for two days without being discovered. And you listened, and your eyes shone, and I felt that you had even made the little Christmas tree listen too, as in a fairy story.'

But of that evening she had remembered a little pot of caviare. It had cost seven and sixpence. He could not get over it. Think of it – a tiny jar like that costing seven and sixpence. While she ate it he watched her, delighted and shocked.

'No, really, that is eating money. You could not get seven shillings into a little pot that size. Only think of the profit they must make . . .' And he had begun some immensely complicated calculations . . . But now goodbye to the caviare. The Christmas tree was on the table, and the little boy lay under the cart with his head pillowed on the yard dog.

'The dog was called Bosun,' she cried delightedly.

But he did not follow. 'Which dog? Had you a dog? I don't remember a dog at all.'

'No, no. I mean the yard dog when you were a little boy.' He laughed and snapped the cigarette-case to.

'Was he? Do you know I had forgotten that. It seems such ages ago. I cannot believe that it is only six years. After I had recognised you today – I had to take such a leap – I had to take a leap over my whole life to get back to that time. I was such a kid then.' He drummed on the table. 'I've often thought how I must have bored you. And now I understand so perfectly why you wrote to me as you did – although at the time that letter nearly finished my life. I found it again the other day, and I couldn't help laughing as I read it. It was so clever – such a true picture of me.' He glanced up. 'You're not going?'

She had buttoned her collar again and drawn down her veil.

'Yes, I am afraid I must,' she said, and managed a smile. Now she knew that he had been mocking.

'Ah no, please,' he pleaded. 'Don't go just for a moment,' and he caught up one of her gloves from the table and clutched at it as if that would hold her. 'I see so few people to talk to nowadays, that I have turned into a sort of barbarian,' he said. 'Have I said something to hurt you?'

'Not a bit,' she lied. But as she watched him draw her glove through his fingers, gently, gently, her anger really did die down, and besides, at the moment he looked more like himself of six years ago . . .

'What I really wanted then,' he said softly, 'was to be a sort of carpet – to make myself into a sort of carpet for you to walk on so that you need not be hurt by the sharp stones and the mud that you hated so. It was nothing more positive than that – nothing more selfish. Only I did desire, eventually, to turn into a magic carpet and carry you away to all those lands you longed to see.'

As he spoke she lifted her head as though she drank something; the strange beast in her bosom began to purr . . .

'I felt that you were more lonely than anybody else in the world,' he went on, 'and yet, perhaps, that you were the only person in the world who was really, truly alive. Born out of your time,' he murmured, stroking the glove, 'fated.'

Ah, God! What had she done! How had she dared to throw away her happiness like this. This was the only man who had ever understood her. Was it too late? Could it be too late? *She* was that glove that he held in his fingers . . .

'And then the fact that you had no friends and never had made friends with people. How I understood that, for neither had I. Is it just the same now?'

'Yes,' she breathed. 'Just the same. I am as alone as ever.'

'So am I,' he laughed gently, 'just the same.'

Suddenly with a quick gesture he handed her back the glove and scraped his chair on the floor. 'But what seemed to me so mysterious then is perfectly plain to me now. And to you, too, of course . . . It simply was that we were such egoists, so self-engrossed, so wrapped up in ourselves that we hadn't a corner in our hearts for anybody else. Do you know,' he cried, naïve and hearty, and dreadfully like another side of that old self again, 'I began studying a Mind System when I was in Russia, and I found that we were not peculiar at all. It's quite a well-known form of . . .'

She had gone. He sat there, thunder-struck, astounded beyond words . . . And then he asked the waitress for his bill.

'But the cream has not been touched,' he said. 'Please do not charge me for it.'

Widowed

They came down to breakfast next morning absolutely their own selves. Rosy, fresh, and just chilled enough by the cold air blowing through the bedroom windows to be very ready for hot coffee.

'Nippy.' That was Geraldine's word as she buttoned on her orange coat with pink-washed fingers. 'Don't you find it decidedly nippy?' And her voice, so matter-of-fact, so natural, sounded as though they had been married for years.

Parting his hair with two brushes (marvellous feat for a woman to watch) in the little round mirror, he had replied, lightly clapping the brushes together, 'My dear, have you got enough *on?*' and he, too, sounded as though well he knew from the experience of years her habit of clothing herself underneath in wisps of chiffon and two satin bows . . . Then they ran down to breakfast, laughing together and terribly startling the shy parlour-maid who, after talking it over with Cook, had decided to be invisible until she was rung for.

'Good morning, Nellie, I think we shall want more toast than *that*,' said the smiling Geraldine as she hung over the breakfast table. She deliberated – 'Ask Cook to make us four more pieces, please.'

Marvellous, the parlour-maid thought it was. And

as she closed the door she heard the voice say, 'I do so hate to be short of toast, don't you?'

He was standing in the sunny window. Geraldine went up to him. She put her hand on his arm and gave it a gentle squeeze. How pleasant it was to feel that rough man's-tweed again. Ah, how pleasant! She rubbed her hand against it, touched it with her cheek, sniffed the smell.

The window looked out on to flower beds, a tangle of Michaelmas daisies, late dahlias, hanging heavy, and shaggy little asters. Then there came a lawn strewn with yellow leaves with a broad path beyond and a row of gold-fluttering trees. An old gardener, in woollen mitts, was sweeping the path, brushing the leaves into a neat little heap. Now, the broom tucked in his arm, he fumbled in his coat pocket, brought out some matches, and scooping a hole in the leaves he set fire to them.

Such lovely blue smoke came breathing into the air through those dry leaves; there was something so calm and orderly in the way the pile burned that it was a pleasure to watch. The old gardener stumped away and came back with a handful of withered twigs. He flung them on and stood by, and little light flames began to flicker.

'I do think,' said Geraldine, 'I do think there is nothing nicer than a real satisfactory fire.'

'Jolly, isn't it,' he murmured back, and they went to their first breakfast.

Just over a year ago, thirteen months, to be exact, she had been standing before the dining-room window of the little house in Sloane Street. It looked over the railed gardens. Breakfast was over, cleared away and done with . . . she had a fat bunch of letters in her hand that she meant to answer, snugly, over the fire. But before settling down, the autumn sun, the freshness had drawn her to the window. Such a perfect morning for the Row. Jimmie had gone riding.

'Goodbye, dear thing.'

'Goodbye, Gerry mine.' And then the morning kiss, quick and firm. He looked so handsome in his riding kit. She imagined him as she stood there . . . riding. Geraldine was not very good at imagining things. But there was mist, a thud of hooves and Jimmie's moustache was damp. From the garden there sounded the creak of a gardener's barrow. An old man came into sight with a load of leaves and a broom lying across. He stopped; he began to sweep. 'What enormous tufts of irises grew in London gardens,' mused Geraldine. 'Why?' And now the smoke of a real fire ascended.

'There is nothing nicer,' she thought, 'than a really satisfactory fire.'

Just at that moment the telephone bell rang. Geraldine sat down at Jimmie's desk to answer it. It was Major Hunter.

'Good morning, Major. You're a very early bird!'

'Good morning, Mrs Howard. Yes. I am.' (Geraldine made a little surprised face at herself. How odd he sounded!) 'Mrs Howard, I'm coming round to see you . . . now . . . I'm taking a taxi . . . Please don't go out. And – and –' the voice stammered, 'p-please don't let the servants go out.'

'*Par*-don?' This last was so very peculiar, though the whole thing had been peculiar enough, that Geraldine couldn't believe what she heard. But he was gone. He had rung off. What on earth – and putting down the receiver, she took up a pencil and drew what she always drew when she sat down before a piece of blotting-paper – the behind of a little cat with whiskers and tail complete. Geraldine must have drawn that little cat hundreds of times, all over the world, in hotels, in clubs, at steamer desks, waiting at the bank. The little cat was her sign, her mark. She had copied it from a little girl at school when she thought it most wonderful. And she never tried anything else. She was . . . not very good at drawing. This particular cat was drawn with an extra firm pen and even its whiskers looked surprised.

'Not to let the servants go out!' But she had never heard anything so peculiar in her life. She must have made a mistake. Geraldine couldn't help a little giggle of amusement. And why should he tell her he was taking a taxi? And why – above all – should he be coming to see her at that hour of the morning?

Then – it came over her – like a flash she remembered Major Hunter's mania for old furniture. They had been discussing it at the Carlton the last time they lunched together. And he had said something to Jimmie about some – Jacobean or Queen Anne – Geraldine knew nothing about these things – something or other. Could he possibly be bringing it round? But of course. He must be. And that explained the remark about the servants. He wanted them to help getting it into the house. What a bore! Geraldine did hope it would tone in. And really, she must say she thought Major Hunter was taking a good deal for granted to produce a thing that size at that hour of the day without a word of warning. They hardly knew him well enough for that. Why make such a mystery of it too? Geraldine hated mysteries. But she had heard his head was rather troublesome at times ever since the Somme affair. Perhaps this was one of his bad days. In that case, a pity Jimmie was not back. She rang. Mullins answered.

'Oh, Mullins, I'm expecting Major Hunter in a few moments. He's bringing something rather heavy. He may want you to help with it. And Cook had better be ready too.'

Geraldine's manner was slightly lofty with her servants. She enjoyed carrying things off with a high hand. All the same, Mullins did look surprised. She seemed to hover for a moment before she went out. It annoyed Geraldine greatly. What was there to be surprised at? What could have been simpler? she thought, sitting down to her batch of letters, and the fire, and the clock and her pen began to whisper together.

There was the taxi – making an enormous noise at the door. She thought she heard the driver's voice too, arguing. It took her a long moment to clasp her writing-case and to get up out of the low chair. The bell rang. She went straight to the dining-room door –

And there was Major Hunter in his riding kit, coming quickly towards her, and behind him, through the open door at the bottom of the steps, she saw something big, something grey. It was an ambulance.

'There's been an accident,' cried Geraldine sharply.

'Mrs Howard.' Major Hunter ran forward. He put out his icy cold hand and wrung hers. 'You'll be brave, won't you?' he said, he pleaded.

But of course she would be brave.

'Is it serious?'

Major Hunter nodded gravely. He said the one word 'Yes.'

'Very serious?'

Now he raised his head. He looked her full in the eyes. She'd never realised until that moment that he was extraordinarily handsome though in a melodrama kind of way. 'It's as bad as it can be, Mrs Howard,' said Major Hunter simply. 'But – go in there,' he said hastily, and he almost pushed her into her own dining-room. 'We must bring him in – where can we –'

'Can he be taken upstairs?' asked Geraldine.

'Yes, yes, of course.' Major Hunter looked at her so strangely – so painfully.

'There's his dressing-room,' said Geraldine. 'It's on the first floor. I'll lead the way,' and she put her hand on the Major's arm. 'It's quite all right, Major,' she said, 'I'm not going to break down –' and she actually smiled, a confident brilliant smile.

To her amazement, as Major Hunter turned away he burst out with, 'Ah, my God! I'm so sorry.'

Poor man. He was quite overcome. 'Brandy after-wards,' thought Geraldine. 'Not now, of course.'

It was a painful moment when she heard those measured deliberate steps in the hall. But Geraldine, realising this was not the moment, and there was nothing to be gained by it, refrained from looking.

'This way, Major.' She skimmed on in front, up the stairs, along the passage; she flung open the door of Jimmie's gay, living, breathing dressing-room and stood to one side – for Major Hunter, for the two stretcher-bearers. Only then she realised that it must be a scalp wound – some injury to the head. For there was nothing to be seen of Jimmie; the sheet was pulled right over . . .

THE STORY OF PENGUIN CLASSICS

Before 1946 ...'Classics' are mainly the domain of academics and students, without readable editions for everyone else. This all changes when a little-known classicist, E. V. Rieu, presents Penguin founder Allen Lane with the translation of Homer's Odyssey that he has been working on and reading to his wife Nelly in his spare time.

1946 The Odyssey becomes the first Penguin Classic published, and promptly sells three million copies. Suddenly, classic books are no longer for the privileged few.

1950s Rieu, now series editor, turns to professional writers for the best modern, readable translations, including Dorothy L. Sayers's *Inferno* and Robert Graves's *The Twelve Caesars*, which revives the salacious original.

1960s 1961 sees the arrival of the Penguin Modern Classics, showcasing the best twentieth-century writers from around the world. Rieu retires in 1964, hailing the Penguin Classics list as 'the greatest educative force of the 20th century'.

1970s A new generation of translators arrives to swell the Penguin Classics ranks, and the list grows to encompass more philosophy, religion, science, history and politics.

1980s The Penguin American Library joins the Classics stable, with titles such as *The Last of the Mohicans* safeguarded. Penguin Classics now offers the most comprehensive library of world literature available.

1990s Penguin Popular Classics are launched, offering readers budget editions of the greatest works of literature. Penguin Audiobooks brings the classics to a listening audience for the first time, and in 1999 the launch of the Penguin Classics website takes them online to an ever larger global readership.

The 21st Century Penguin Classics are rejacketed for the first time in nearly twenty years. This world famous series now consists of more than 1,300 titles, making the widest range of the best books ever written available to millions – and constantly redefining the meaning of what makes a 'classic'.

The Odyssey continues ...

The best books ever written

PENGUIN CLASSICS

SINCE 1946

Find out more at www.penguinclassics.com